Dear Reader

Welcome to thi[...]
author Jennifer [...]
the joy—and the anxiety—unplanned parenthood
can bring, and introduces a couple whose lives
change as they prepare for their new arrival.

Adrienne Bennett is totally surprised, and a little
panicky, when she discovers she's pregnant.
Naturally, she's also concerned about the reaction
of the baby's father, Riley Stuart. Fortunately,
Riley responds by buying armfuls of baby
manuals and starting to plan their future together!

Enjoy!

The Editors

Riley's Baby

JENNIFER
GREENE

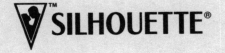

*Silhouette and Colophon are registered trademarks of
Harlequin Books S.A., used under licence.*

*First published in Great Britain 1992
Silhouette Books, Eton House, 18-24 Paradise Road,
Richmond, Surrey TW9 1SR*

© Jennifer Greene 1990

Originally published in Birds, Bees and Babies
© Silhouette Books 1990

ISBN 0 373 59691 X

54-9905

*Printed and bound in Great Britain
by Caledonian International Book Manufacturing Ltd, Glasgow*

A Note from Jennifer Greene

I love babies. If there are forty adults and a baby in the room, I inevitably gravitate towards the baby.

My love of babies is no way a measure of my ability to raise them. My husband and I have two children. Ryan was a brilliant and precocious baby. He decided, coming out of the womb, that there were strategic times to cry—like whenever I needed to eat or sleep. I can remember adjusting our dinner hours anywhere from three minutes past lunch to 10:00 p.m. It didn't matter; that first wail would kick in as soon as I picked up my fork. I can also remember, many nights, vacuuming my living room carpet at three in the morning with Ryan in my arms. (He slept wonderfully until I turned the vacuum off.)

When Jennifer was born, I was older, tougher, wiser. I threw out the seventeen childcare books I'd read for Ryan and started right in the hospital with lies and bribery. 'If you don't cry for the next fifteen minutes, I'll hold you for the next forty-eight hours straight,' I'd promise her. It didn't do any good. She had me figured out before we left the delivery room.

It's a miracle that my children survived their babyhood. Both kids knew I couldn't stand to hear them cry. Both, accurately, played me for a sucker early on.

I'm just as much a sucker for a love story and always have been. Love stories involving motherhood, though, reach me like no others.

Motherhood is mystical, special, timeless, wonderful. It also takes you out of yourself. Selfishness doesn't survive a baby. If a relationship has holes, they get bigger with the advent of nappies. Babies have a way of putting a major dent in candlelit dinners, champagne and spontaneous lovemaking.

From where I'm sitting, though, motherhood can be the starting point for the greatest romance a woman can have.

When you have a child, you put a different value on love. When you have a child, you test everything you've ever believed about love…because you have to. You have to fight for the time to be together; you have to find something to give when you're as limp as a dishrag; you have to be understanding when your sole goal in life is burying your head under a pillow for eight hours of uninterrupted sleep.

That kind of love takes work—lots more work than a candlelit dinner—but in the process you build something as strong as cement. Real love, tough love, the kind that hurts, the kind that matters, the kind that lasts—this is magic of the most powerful kind.

My story is not about a married couple, but a single one. They *have* love…but not a love that's been tested yet. There's no cement. Their whole concept of romance is the magic created when the two of them are alone together. They think that's all there is. They don't know how big, how strong, how powerful the scope of love can really be. They're just starting their real romance, but they'll have to discover that for themselves.

Jennifer Greene

Prologue

Mary smoothed, folded and tucked with an efficiency the army would have admired. Technically it was the nurses aide's job to make the bed, not hers. Just as technically, of course, it was a doctor's job to deliver babies, but Mary had delivered her share for more than twenty years. Hospital administrators liked to make rules and regulations and policies. She'd been a nurse too long to pay much attention.

She finished with the bed and straightened, her eyes narrowing on the rest of the room. It didn't look like much—just a bed, monitor, table/tray and a worn out Naugahyde chair squeezed into the corner. The clanking radiator didn't add much to the decor; neither did the faded green paint on the walls. Most would say the room looked barren and sterile, emotionless.

They'd be dead wrong.

Junction General Hospital was too small to have a formal labor room. Room 232, at the end of the hall, was reserved for expectant mothers. Mary personally made the bed in the room. She also personally ensured that no dust touched the windowsill, no water spots marred the sink in the bathroom, no crease disturbed the smooth white cotton blanket.

Bringing life into this world was a hard and intimately personaly business. Mary knew—she'd done it five times herself—and over the years she'd watched the times change.

Twenty years ago a mother was sedated almost upon arrival. Now a woman in labor rarely received any drug unless it was absolutely necessary.

Twenty years ago, almost every mother was married—and nearly every father was shooed to the waiting room. Now, mothers delivering for the first time were just as likely to be fourteen as forty. No one asked if they were married, and fathers—wed or not—were often enough part of the birth.

Twenty years ago, the women wore the earrings. Now, heaven knew, the fathers occasionally did. At least in one ear.

Mary fiddled with the backs of her own earrings— red garnet studs inherited from her great-grandmother, and her only vanity. She heard herself being paged, strode for the door and hesitated. She gave the room one last glance to make sure it was right—not right and prepared by anyone else's standards, but by her own. It could be days before a young woman was admitted to this room. It could be minutes.

Maybe the details of life had changed over the years, but some things never did. Babies were always going to arrive in their own good time, and never conveniently. Expectant fathers were always going to be more difficult to deal with than the mothers, and it took pain to deliver a baby. No philosophy or pain killer or Lamaze classes were ever going to change that.

Mary heard her name paged again, yet she still

didn't move. She'd seen more than twenty years of babies born in this room. Twenty years of life—and love—and stories she'd never told and never would tell.

Those stories had given her a different perspective than most. If anyone asked Mary—and no one ever had—the cycle of romance didn't start with Adam and Eve and an apple, but nine months later. Stories of birth were stories of searing privacy, unforgettable pain, joy, anticipation, fear that tore at a soul…and the renewal of birth that mended it.

Room 232 wasn't just a place. It was a moment in time, in which two people had the chance to experience the ultimate romance of love and life. A moment in time when a man and a woman could make or break each other. Mary had seen it go both ways.

Certainly babies were a jolt of reality, between diapers and night feedings and burpings and colic. Giving birth, though, was the single greatest jolt of reality there was. This was it. Everything that mattered. And either the right kind of love went into the making of a baby, or it didn't.

The prices were all paid here. In room 232.

Chapter One

"You're pregnant."

"I can't be." Adrienne Bennett's voice was quite firm.

The doctor stepped away and plucked at her vinyl glove. "About eight weeks along."

"I *can't* be."

"My guess is early December—"

"My guess is that you have the wrong rabbit, because mine couldn't have died." Adrienne lifted her feet from the blasted stirrups. The paper blanket tried to flutter to the floor. Agitated, she grabbed it. "Come on, Liz. I'm thirty-three years old, which you know as well as you know me. I've never believed in luck, never played Russian roulette, and I sure as heck have never been careless about birth control. *Never.*"

Dr. Liz Conklin reached for a pen and the prescription pad, but her gaze focused on her old friend. She wasn't fooled by Adrienne's exasperated attempt at humor. "Take it easy," she advised. "These things happen no matter how careful a woman is. Give yourself a chance to get used to the idea before you panic."

Panic wasn't even a word in Adrienne's vocabulary. Or it didn't used to be. "Two thousand years of medical science. They cured polio. They can give you a new heart. So how is it that we're about to reach the twenty-first century without a foolproof method to guard against pregnancy? It's unbelievable!''

''Riley won't be half as upset as you are,'' Liz said calmly.

''Riley will divorce me,'' Adrienne immediately contradicted her.

''He can't divorce you. You aren't married.''

''Which is far worse. If you're married and surprised by a pregnancy, that's one thing. If you're just living together, that's another. Riley didn't sign on for this kind of complication.''

''Neither did you, but this kind of 'complication' takes two. I'm almost sure that our mutually favorite industrial relations attorney has a good idea how babies are made. He also happens to worship the ground you walk on. You don't suppose there's a chance—a slim, remote chance—that Riley won't be half as upset as you are?''

Because Liz was trying to be soothing, Adrienne wanted to make a light comeback, but couldn't. Her whole body was cold—chill cold, fear cold. Her heart felt as heavy as lead. She was famous for her sense of humor, but couldn't dredge up an ounce of it now. Babies were a subject she had always taken very, very seriously, which was the precise reason she had been so careful to never become pregnant.

All Adrienne had to do was close her eyes to conjure up a mental picture of Riley. The cliché about tall, dark and handsome had probably started with him. So did the one about electric blue eyes. But his lethally sexy looks had never captured her attention. She couldn't care less what a man looked like as long as he was compassionate and intelligent and had a long dollop of integrity.

Riley had a long dollop of the devil. Other men had been scared off by her cool reserve. Riley had been amused by it. Most men were predictably threatened by a strong, successful woman. Riley had made Adrienne laugh at herself. *No* man had any difficulty understanding her when she said no and meant it. Riley had taken her no's all the way to bed with them, and then had the unprincipled gall to make the experience so devastating, so delicious, so terrifyingly special that she couldn't think straight.

She'd known from the beginning that he was a flirt with a rogue's reputation. Throw a party, and women tripped over themselves to get to Riley's side. He loved that. The problem with Riley was that he was one of those rare men who honestly liked women. He also knew them. Too well—so well that she'd had a heck of a time covering up her symptoms until she had the chance to make this doctor's appointment. "Look, Liz, there has to be a chance you're wrong. I only missed one period. That happened before, and the only thing wrong was an innocuous little fibroid cyst."

"There's a definite difference between a cyst and a normal, healthy uterus eight weeks into pregnancy." Liz said firmly, "Knowing you, you guessed you were pregnant before you walked in, so let's get serious here. I want to do some blood work and get

you on some vitamins, and you're built on the small
side, kiddo, meaning that your pelvis isn't equipped
to take a watermelon. With very careful control of the
baby's weight, you shouldn't have any major problems.''

"Believe me, I have a *major* problem."

"Talk to Riley."

"I—"

"Adrienne, go home and talk with Riley!"

At five minutes to twelve Adrienne, dressed in a
red blouse and businesslike white suit, was standing
at a pharmacist's window with a handful of prescriptions. Somewhere behind the counter, there was an
open bottle of alcohol. The odor made her stomach
roll. *Talk to Riley?*

Once her prescriptions for vitamins were filled, she
walked into an adjoining deli to grab a quick sand-
wich. The tantalizing aroma of corn beef made her
mouth water, but the same smell made her stomach
pitch acid. She quickly walked out again. The first
day of April was balmy and redolent with the scents
of spring. She didn't notice. *How could she possibly
talk to Riley?*

It was only a short fifteen-minute drive through
midtown Indianapolis to the law offices of Reeder,
Small and Burkholtz. It wasn't fair. The moment she
stepped in the door, she was starving to death. The
coffee room only yielded a box of stale crackers,
which she munched frantically before her first afternoon client.

The firm's specialty was divorce, and if Adrienne

continued her success rate with clients, Reeder, Small and Burkholtz were going to be stuck adding "Bennett" to the partnership. The boys may have hired her with all the right mumbo jumbo slogans about equality, but Adrienne knew the score. They never really thought she'd cut it. Women attorneys didn't abound in divorce. The field was too ugly and too tough.

At one o'clock, she heard out the ravings of an embittered wife who'd stayed in an abusive relationship too long. Her second client of the afternoon was a man, who was determined to take his unfaithful wife for everything she had right down to her false eyelashes.

Both cases were ugly; both were tough. Adrienne's colleagues claimed that no divorce attorney sustained any ideals or romantic illusions for long. Luckily she'd never started with any romantic illusions, but ideals were another story. She had specifically chosen divorce as her legal specialty because of an ideal: to help people get divorced as painlessly as possible.

Her parents were one of those unfortunate couples who never had the good sense to get a divorce. As in most marriages, it took two to tango. Her father was certainly guilty of numerous infidelities...but her mother had incomparable skill at saying just the right thing at just the right time to wound and emasculate. As far as Adrienne could tell, the two had spent thirty-five years living to hurt each other.

At five o'clock, she left a desk full of work and took her queasy stomach home. Her work as a divorce attorney only reaffirmed values she'd learned as a child. Love was a powerful and positive force. Marriage, regrettably, had nothing to do with love. Enter possessiveness and ties and forced responsibilities, and the relationship went *"pffft."* Every time.

The exhaust fumes on the expressway nearly took her stomach out for good. Riley knew exactly how she felt about marriage. Everyone argued in a relationship—an occasional spat was the spice of life—but the only times they'd ended up shouting at each other was about marriage. Riley had finally, permanently, dropped the subject.

Adrienne was terrified it would come up again when he discovered she was pregnant.

Either that, or he'd walk out on her.

In her head, she knew Riley wasn't the kind of man to walk out on any woman in trouble. But in her heart, Adrienne had been waiting for Riley to walk out from the day she'd met him. Men liked soft women. She wasn't soft. She was terribly hard and terribly cynical and cold—good grief, at five years old she'd had to learn to be cold!—but Riley just didn't seem to see her that way.

Riley might be the best thing that had ever happened to her, but a pregnancy changed everything. Their whole relationship was based on mutual needs and matched respect and sharing—not dependence. Never dependence. Adrienne knew precisely what happened to a relationship when either partner was cornered into forced feelings of responsibility. The result was shambles.

Talk to Riley, Liz had advised. Well, she would.

She'd talk tough, blunt, practical, hardheaded common sense; she'd make absolutely positive he was off the hook. Blunt, tough realism came naturally to her. The talk wouldn't be any problem at all.

A horn blared from the merging lane of the freeway. She hadn't seen the aging Chevy. Her eyes had been too filled with tears.

Swinging a briefcase full of labor contracts, Riley ignored the elevator and took the stairs two at a time. He'd missed his morning jog as well as his usual half hour on the handball court at lunch. The only muscles he'd used all day had been in his rear end. Every nerve was singing with pent-up physical energy.

Halfway down the hall, he dug into his pants pocket for the apartment key. He was whistling when Mrs. McFadden stepped outside her door for the evening paper, dressed in a housecoat that barely camouflaged her Buddha-like rolls. He winked a hello at her, and she blushed to the roots of her newly tinted pink hair.

You still got it, Riley. At least with the geriatric set. He was laughing at himself when he turned the key, then mentally swore when he discovered he'd locked the door, not unlocked it. Adrienne regularly promised to lock herself in when she arrived home first. She never remembered. She also never remembered to fill her car with gas, that food was required sustenance for all human beings, and that he really did hate perfumed soap.

None of those monumental faults had ever affected

his feelings for her. Dropping his briefcase, he pushed off his shoes and shrugged out of his suit coat. Adrienne had decorated the place, which was why there was a brass rack and table waiting for the debris he inevitably stashed at the door.

"Adrienne?" Ambling through the hallway, he peered into the kitchen—a study in oak, stained glass, and leftover-breakfast coffee cups.

She wasn't there, nor was she in the second bedroom they'd turned into a study. The matching desks were empty, the bookshelves untouched. He'd argued with her about using "midnight blue" paint because the room was already dark, but as usual, Adrienne was right. Coupled with soft light, her "blues" made for a restful, serene work area for both of them in an evening.

The hall took a turn and twist before reaching the living room. Unlike the dark blue study, she'd made their living area all light and color.

The overstuffed couch and chairs were man-size, in deference to his six-two frame, but the splashes of feminine color were uniquely Adrienne. No question she liked spice, and the contemporary oil over the white marble fireplace picked up her favorite paprika, cinnamon and vanilla. The tables were brass and glass, relieved from a cold contemporary look by textures. The coffee table sat on a thick white fur rug. She'd hung South American *molas* on the far wall. Adrienne was a big believer in pillows—huge, fat ones, the kind a man could sink his head in after a long, hard day.

Every time he walked in, he remembered how much he'd hated the singles scene and coming home to a bleak, cold apartment alone. Adrienne had done more than change the colors; she had ruthlessly altered the place until a man found comfort in every niche and corner. She was a hopeless nurturer—a label Riley knew she would promptly and pithily deny.

He spotted her from the doorway. She obviously hadn't heard him come in because she was slouched on the couch with her back to him. All he could see was the crown of her head. For a moment he paused, wondering—not for the first time—why he'd had to fall for such a complex and troublesome woman.

Adrienne didn't look like trouble, and he happened to know her body intimately well. She was built lithe and long, with legs that didn't end and hips so small they were swallowed in jeans. She had no vanity. Her breasts came right out of a man's fantasy. They weren't big. Just firm, white and responsive, with nipples no bigger than buttons. If you tried to compliment her she'd laughingly exhibit her feet, which she thought were huge. She was wrong.

She'd kissed a dog when she was three, who'd taken a chunk out of her fanny in response. She still had the embarrassing scar. He'd spent a lot of time worrying how many other men had seen that scar, also how many other dogs she'd kissed in the figurative sense. There couldn't have been many because Adrienne was no fool, but something or someone had given her a defensive edge that she never quite lost, a fiercely guarded independence that she never quite forgot.

She cultivated a professional image. Her hairstyle was short and sassy, just a thick swirl of chestnut with a sweep of bangs on one side. She inevitably chose clothes that tooted the same picture—bright, quick, practical and capable. Her self-image, although inarguably accurate to a point, was not at all how Riley saw her.

More than once, he'd mused that he'd like to get her in front of a mirror and show her the Adrienne that he knew. Drowning soft brown eyes. Fragile, translucent skin. Small lips that could readily be coaxed to laughter and an irreverently tipped nose. She walked with an exuberance, just a bit of a feminine swish that advertised confidence in her own sexuality. Riley loved that feminine swish, even recognizing it for the storefront it was.

No human being on this earth could be more easily hurt than Adrienne.

Riley soundlessly walked up behind her and leaned over. He barely caught the startled flash of surprise in her eyes before sealing his mouth over hers. Beyond a first taste of something unexpectedly cold and candylike on her lips, reality disappeared for several moments after that. It always did when he kissed Adrienne.

Her scent had seduced him first. She liked perfumes that drove a man crazy, a hint of soft dare, a hint of something elusive and teasing. It was the first thing he'd noticed about her, the first thing that made him decide she was bad news and better avoided. The second thing he'd noticed was how she kissed. Adrienne melted in layers, first an extraordinary shyness, then warmth, then a layer of yielding and yearning passion that went straight to a man's head.

After their first kiss, he'd cut her from the pack of men who used to surround her as relentlessly as a stag isolated his chosen doe in the fall.

Adrienne hadn't been easy to corner. She was even tougher to protect, partly because she considered herself one tough self-reliant cookie. And partly because Adrienne, from the first, had turned his world upside down. Riley wasn't a stranger to a love affair, and most women found him laid back, accepting, easy to be with. Not violently protective. Not caveman-possessive. Never aggravated. Never stressed to the absolute limit of his patience, which used to be considerable. And never turned on to the point of madness by the simplest kisses. Except with Adrienne.

After a year and a half he should have been used to her ability to surprise him, but tonight was different yet again. When he'd leaned over her, all he'd intended was a peck, a simple "hi, love" smooch.

It started that way. But *she* was the one who twisted around so her arms could sweep around his neck. Her head tilted to encourage the crush of his mouth. He crushed, obliging her. Desire sliced through him, fueled by her warmth and willingness. Adrienne could take when coaxed. She rarely demanded, yet her fingers speared through his hair, anchoring him still, ensuring his closeness.

Her skin smelled like the lilac soap he hated on him, and adored on her. So soft. He found her tongue. Her response was wild, deliciously desperate, a murmur lost between them and treasured more than she knew, but his thumb abruptly discovered that the pulse in her throat was trembling.

It took him another minute to realize that she was trembling all over.

Startled, he pulled back—not urgently and not far. With his palm still cupped in her hair, he murmured teasingly, "Hey, that was quite a homecoming welcome."

No one could jump out of emotional waters faster than Adrienne. "I don't suppose you'd believe that I thought you were the mailman?"

"No."

"Ah, well. I suppose it must have been you I was glad to see."

"Rough day?"

"Long and traumatic," she admitted blithely.

He could see that—now. In fact, on a mental level the red phone just rang in his personal White House. There were no tears in her eyes, but her lashes were damp. He'd never seen Adrienne cry, and the lamplight was too dim to guarantee he wasn't misreading the faintest redness in her eyes. Confusing him further was the package on her lap. Unless he was having hallucinations, she was holding a spoon and a pint of fast-melting butter brickle ice cream.

"Since when..." he began.

"Oh, quit grinning at me, Riley. I saw it was on

sale at the convenience store at the corner and wandered in. I haven't had butter brickle since I was a kid. It's unbelievably good,'' she said feelingly, and as lithe as a cat—as if nothing was wrong—swung off the couch.

"You actually polished off an entire pint?"

"It's not like junk food. Ice cream is absolutely loaded with nutritional things. Like calcium—"

"And butter brickle." When he swung an arm around her to steer her toward the kitchen, he knew for sure she'd cried. He also knew he wasn't going to get anything out of her until she was good and ready. Adrienne could be pushed—about as easily as a mountain. "I don't suppose you're in the least hungry for some real dinner after your...um... appetizer?"

"Are you kidding? I could eat half a whale."

Again he paused. For the past two weeks, Adrienne's appetite had rivaled that of a hummingbird's. Further, she never went on an eating binge without reason. He considered whether Burkholtz had put the move on her, whether one of the custody issues she handled involved an abused child, or whether her mother had called. "Anything interesting happen today?" he asked casually.

"First thing this morning I had the meeting with the Laughlins. Property settlement, I told you? They argued over every spoon and ashtray."

"Stressful?"

"Not really. More humorous, particularly when

they got to the ashtrays.'' She looked up with a dry grin. ''Neither of them even smoke.''

''Burkholtz hit you with the review schedule?'' He knew the issue of her potential partnership would come up with the spring review.

''No time, never even saw him today. How about you? How'd the meeting go with the union lawyer from U.B.R.?''

He followed up with chitchat, keeping a careful eye on her at the same time. Letting Adrienne loose in a kitchen had similar repercussions to giving an untrained puppy the run of the house. Riley had learned a long time ago to give her some innocuously harmless task—like tossing salad.

In principle, it wasn't fair to give her anything to do. They split the chores. He did the cooking and the laundry. She did the shopping, cleaning and taxes. He had no problem with the fair division of labor; it was Adrienne who got the feminine guilts when he worked in the kitchen.

As he sautéed the chicken breasts, he only hoped her problem *was* the feminine guilts. She was shredding lettuce into bits too microscopic to see. ''Your mother call you?'' he asked lightly.

''No. Why should she—Riley, don't.''

''Don't what?'' His white shirt cuffed to the elbows, he was cleaning the season's first asparagus under the open faucet.

''Not asparagus. Not tonight.''

He raised a brow. ''You love asparagus. It's your favorite—''

"*Please.* Not asparagus."

Adrienne didn't have a fussy bone in her body, but hey, everyone had an occasional whim. By the time he'd rearranged the menu to cater to her appetite, though, dinner had deteriorated into bland chicken, dull peas and plain old potatoes. She managed the peas, pushed the rest around her plate, and finished off with a slice of unbuttered bread. The half a glass of wine he poured her remained untouched. She wanted milk. They'd lived together for a year and a half. She'd never wanted milk.

It was easiest to clean up when there were no leftovers. Heaven knew, he didn't want to save anything from the dinner. He carried and scraped; she rinsed and fed the dishes to the dishwasher, talking shop at the same time. "So Wednesday, I'm probably going to be stuck in court all day. The custody hearing's going to take all of the afternoon. I've been looking forward to coming up against Dailey for a long time. If he thinks he's going to win one off his reputation this time, he's living in a dream world. How do you feel about abortion, Riley?"

"Pardon?" Last he knew, she was discussing hanging a fellow attorney out to dry.

"Abortion. I'm just curious how you feel about it. I never happened to ask you." Her back was to him. She'd taken a glass out of the cupboard and was holding it to the light. Adrienne hated water spots. "Are you for it or against it?"

"Well…" He swiped at the table, his eyes on her back. "Overall, I'm against abortion ever having been made into a legal issue. I think it's a mistake to pretend we can legislate morals and ethics, nor does the legal system have any business intruding on people's individual personal and religious beliefs—''

"Stash it, Riley. I wasn't asking for a courtroom speech. I was just curious how you felt on the subject.''

She was still holding up that glass. At least, until he came up behind her and stole it from her hand. He couldn't identify the emotion rolling in his stomach, but he had the abrupt sensation of falling in quicksand—as if the rest of his life could be affected by the next few seconds and he didn't know any of the parameters, the edges, the rules.

That feeling intensified when he turned Adrienne around by applying gentle pressure to her shoulders. He only caught the briefest glimpse of her eyes—she lowered them too quickly—but there was time enough. His so "tough," so sassy, so fiercely controlled Adrienne was scared. The look in her eyes was as haunted and desperate as a cornered doe's.

"So..." he said softly. "We're pregnant, are we?"

Chapter Two

Riley's voice was tender, but Adrienne saw what mattered. His whole body had locked still and his eyes were a blank, stunned blue.

She had never expected him to react with a delirious whoop of joy—good grief, neither of them wanted a pregnancy—yet her heartbeat suddenly dragged and she was curiously tempted to cry. Silly weakness. When his hands tightened on her shoulders, she firmly ducked from the contact and averted her eyes. "*We* are not pregnant, Riley. That's a medical and metaphysical impossibility. I'm the only one pregnant. This is my problem, not yours."

"I believe it takes two."

She was ready for that. "And that would have stuck you in the hot seat of responsibility if we lived in the eighteenth century. Luckily we live in the twentieth." All Ms. Efficiency, she hung up the dish towel and punched the button to start the dishwasher. "It doesn't take two people to handle the problem these days. I know you don't want a baby—"

"Actually, I don't believe we've ever discussed it," Riley said quietly. "Come here, honey."

She didn't want to "come here." If she came anywhere near him, she was positive she would do something stupid, like drape herself all over him, or worse, cry. Besides, the kitchen was clean. She shut off the lights and strolled to their bedroom as if it were any other night. After dinner, she always fed the fish.

The aquariums took up one whole wall in their sea-blue bedroom, and she didn't need to turn on the overhead because the tanks were illuminated. Silver dollars swam over iridescent stones in one tank; angel fish danced near the bubbler in another; and the last held a school of darting, bright neons. Riley had bought the first pair of fish, but Adrienne was the one who'd expanded their shared hobby—not because she was so crazy about fish, but for a far more private reason. Romance. He would surely laugh at her if he knew—the whole world knew she didn't have a romantic bone in her body!—but she had a hundred memories of Riley, naked, his skin catching the light and shadow of shimmering reflections, his whispers backdropped by the muted sound of bubbling water, his eyes and hands…

She stiffened when she realized he'd followed her to the doorway. Damn pregnancy hormones. They had her feeling all shaky and vulnerable when she wanted most to be strong—for his sake much more than her own. She fumbled with the cap to the fish food. ''The thing is to stay calm, Riley. At least try to relax! The only way to discuss the problem is logically and rationally, and getting upset doesn't solve anything at all—''

''Honey, I am calm.''

''So am I. Completely.'' Except that she abruptly spilled a tablespoon's worth of fish food in the tank. They were only supposed to be fed a pinch. Frantically she reached for the green scooper. "I've *never* been more calm."

Riley swiped a hand over his face. "Could we backtrack before we have any further discussion on who's calm and who's not? You've been to a doctor. Probably Liz?"

"Yes."

"You're okay? Totally okay, completely healthy?"

"Yes."

"And there's no question—"

"None." She saved the neons and moved on to sprinkle food into the angel fish tank. "Look, I know you can't be happy about this. Neither am I. You signed on for living together, not for this kind of problem—"

"I passed puberty a few years ago. Way back when I was aware that when a man and woman make love—particularly as often as we do—a baby is always a potential repercussion. And that we might have to deal with that, love."

Riley, at his most dangerous, used a certain tone of voice. Adrienne thought of it as his naughty tone, because that same male husky timbre had persuaded her into bed, teased her into trying lobster, and coaxed her into believing that living together was a practical, logical, sensible option. He could magnetize a stone with that voice, and worse than that, he was confusing her. When you drop a bomb like an unexpected pregnancy on a man, surely he should react a little more volatilely than to stand in a doorway and pop a butterscotch?

Unless Riley'd already assumed how they would

handle the problem. Her throat went suddenly dry. "I asked you in the kitchen how you felt about abortion. But I didn't tell you how I feel."

"That wouldn't take a mind reader," he murmured. "You may have never handled an abortion case, but you've taken on more than a few clients involving women's rights, love."

"Yes," she agreed. She was so busy feeding the fish that she couldn't spare a moment to look at him. "The constitutional interpretation of equality affecting women—"

"Is a fine theoretical subject for another night. Tonight we're talking about you. You're sneaking around the fence, Adrienne. It isn't like you. Are you trying to tell me you want an abortion?"

She couldn't answer without facing him. Riley was one of those men who rarely stood still—he was too physical, too full of energy—yet he hadn't budged an inch from the doorway. The aquarium lights made his white shirt look iridescent and harshened his strong-boned face. By contrast, his eyes rested with infinite gentleness on her face, waiting...for an answer she couldn't give him.

She spoke as carefully as if she were tiptoeing through a mine field. "What I'm trying to tell you is that I can't involve you in this choice, Riley. I know that's not fair and I know you don't want a baby and I do care what you feel...but I'm asking you to understand. An abortion is not a choice I can live with, not like this, not for me. I'm sorry."

She had no idea Riley was holding his breath until he closed his eyes and let out a gust of a sigh. With

disorienting speed, he crossed the room and grabbed
on to her. Tightly. So tightly that her cheek felt the
numb of his collar button, and her eyes were on a
level with the pulse beating hard in his throat. Then
her eyes started stinging and her vision blurred into
rainbows. ''I thought you'd be angry,'' she whispered.

''That's pretty obvious.''

''I was positive you would want me to have an
abortion—''

''That's pretty obvious, too, my darling doofus.''

She knew he wanted her to smile. No matter how
serious the subject was, a light touch helped keep
things in perspective—she'd taught him that—but she
couldn't have smiled at the moment if her life de-
pended on it. ''You can't want a baby. You have to
resent the idea.''

''I hadn't planned on one, no. And if you don't
mind, I'd like a little more than ten minutes to get
used to the idea before I comment on babies.''

''You don't have to do that. I've already thought
it out. There's obviously only one answer here, and
that's for me to move out.''

Riley's hands stopped making slow soothing circles
down her spine.

She forged on stubbornly, her cheek still matted
against his shirtfront. ''You talked me into living together, and you did it with logic, Riley. If I remember
right, there came a point where neither of us knew
where our toothbrushes were, where your shirts were
hanging in my closet and my shoes had accumulated
in yours. We couldn't even cook dinner because the

vegetables were all in my fridge and the meat was all in yours—you said it was foolish, and you were right. You said that just because people didn't want to be married shouldn't mean they had to spend a lifetime alone. You said that if our circumstances changed, either of us had the freedom to walk out at any time—''

Riley brushed his lips against her hair. ''Maybe I once said too many things.''

''We made a relationship that freed us both—not tied us down. As far as I know, neither of us have hurt each other, and we've both always been honest.'' She closed her eyes. ''And I'd like to be honest now. You know what I was most afraid of, telling you about the pregnancy?''

''What?''

''That you'd jump in blind with some silly idea about us getting married.''

His hands suddenly clenched a little too roughly on her shoulders. ''That would have been...silly, wouldn't it?''

''You know it would be.''

''I know exactly how you feel about marriage, yes.''

He was holding her far too tightly, but she didn't care. Maybe he'd never hold her this tightly again. No woman held a man by cornering him, and she wouldn't—*couldn't*—do that to Riley. His breath smelled like butterscotch, though, his skin like soap. Both scents were familiar, as familiar as the emotions invoked by his arms around her. He had a gift for making a woman feel protected, cherished, almost—

sometimes—safe. All day long she'd felt so shaky. "If there's no abortion and we're not getting married, that only leaves so many choices, and if I'm going to do the right thing, I have to say that my keeping the baby isn't one of them." She had to gulp to get that land-mind truth out, then rushed on. "The best solution would seem to be adoption."

"Honey—"

"But adoption is not the issue right now—the pregnancy is. Everything's changed now. You know it has. You work for a conservative company—you can't just live with a woman whose stomach is about to swell up like a balloon. It isn't right, and those complications will only get worse, not easier. The obvious answer is for me to move out."

"You're not moving out."

"I really think—"

"Adrienne, would you do me an enormous favor and *quit* thinking? You mind is galloping a hundred miles an hour faster than mine. You may have had a chance to think about this, but I haven't. How about if we leave just a few of these decisions until tomorrow?"

She lifted her head and met his eyes. "Waiting won't change anything. I'm not going to live here and have you grow to resent me. That's what would happen."

"You sound very sure that's what would happen."

"I *am* very sure that's what would happen."

Riley felt as if he'd recently been run over by a semi...and that the offending semi kept backing up for a return hit. He hadn't come in the door expecting to be assaulted with the subjects of pregnancy, babies, abortion and adoption. Even if he had, he'd never found a way to anticipate Adrienne's complex and distinctly feminine mind. For a woman so quick she could probably outthink—and certainly outtalk—Einstein, he was regularly amazed at the insane ideas she could produce from thin air.

For example, that he would ever come to resent her.

She didn't respond to his first kiss. Her head was obviously on babies, not desire. Maybe his head should have been on babies, too, but he'd had his fill of hit-and-run semis for the evening. Babies were an obligingly long nine-month process. Adrienne was upset now. Her eyes were haunted with strain, her face white with tension, and as far as this business of his ever resenting her...she started to say something.

He kissed her again, deeply, thoroughly. His hands slipped behind her to nudge open her skirt button, then handle the zipper at the back. The skirt obligingly whooshed to the floor. Adrienne tried to say something else.

She fired for the feel of his palms cupping her bottom, always had. She liked the earthy rub of his arousal pressed against her, always had. She liked a petal-soft tongue at the base of her throat; she loved her eyes kissed closed; and textures turned her on— his palm skimming her nylon stocking, his hands gliding her silk slip against her skin. It went against everything his feminist and independent lady believed in, but the truth was Adrienne loved being swept away. What she craved even more was being loved.

A fish splashed. Bubbling waters muted the cry of yearning he coaxed from her. By the time she was beneath him on the comforter, she was bare. The aquarium lights pearlized her skin. Her brown eyes were lost, pleading, promising, but it was the hint of despair in those soft eyes that drove him beyond the limits of reason.

A man, at times, simply had to be ruthless about tenderness.

When it was over, she lay shuddering and limp beneath him. "Riley—"

"Sssh." He heard both the bewilderment and confusion in her voice. Neither of them ever got used to it, the explosion of flint and flame whenever they came together, but tonight had even been more. Maybe he should have realized before why her breasts had become so tender, so sensitive. Maybe there was even a medical reason for her heightened desire, her ardent sensuality and uncontrolled responsiveness— namely a pregnancy. He didn't care what the reasons were. She'd come to him like wildfire.

"I don't know what happened. I never expected—"

"Neither did I." His lips found her forehead. "You're beautiful, love. Inside, outside, everywhere."

"I—"

"Sssh." He held her long after she fell asleep. With her eyes closed and her body limp and curled around him, she looked precisely what she was. His lover. His lovely, lonely frightened mate who had spent a childhood and a career surrounded by hurtful relationships.

She had never told him she loved him. For a long time, though, he believed she did, and for just as long he'd known she didn't trust him. For a year and a half, she'd been waiting for his interest to wane, waiting for the explosive passion between them to fizzle, and—most of all—waiting for him to leave her.

No, she didn't tell him any of those things. But a man couldn't live with a woman—not a woman he cared about, not a woman he loved—without gaining some knowledge of how her mind worked. The slightest reference to marriage was enough to raise Adrienne's blood pressure thirty degrees. She would never admit to needing anyone, because that onus would put an invisible rope on the other person's neck. Needing was a capital crime to Adrienne. It was okay for her to take care of him, but she fiercely shielded him from any hint that she might need taking care of, too.

The lady was thirty-three years old. Damn young to be so bullheaded. And damn old to have never had her first experience with trust.

Riley's eyes squeezed tightly in the darkness. He'd always figured he could teach her trust in time. Her pregnancy, though, changed things. He no longer had the luxury of time.

And unless he was extraordinarily careful, he knew darn well he could lose her.

Even before she heard the buzz of the alarm clock, Adrienne knew something was terribly wrong. Her eyes still closed, she rolled over to wrap around Riley for a last-minute snuggle...and discovered him gone, the sheets next to her empty.

Either there had been a tornado, or Indianapolis had had its first earthquake. Riley never woke up before the buzzer. Not that she didn't love him but she knew him. Riley had all the liveliness of a sludge before 9:00 a.m. Worried, Adrienne jerked out of bed, and abruptly felt an attack of dizziness like a bullet of reality. *Yes, you're still pregnant, Miss Bennett.*

She collected a black skirt and white blouse with black piping from the closet, and took her rolling stomach to the bathroom. Even after a fast shower, her reflection in the vanity mirror appalled her. Her cheeks had a glow, her eyes held a sleepy satisfaction, her mouth was a sting of red.

She looked like a woman who had been made love to thoroughly and well—but making love with Riley had not been on the agenda last night. Babies had been. The baby she was not prepared for, the one she was sure he didn't want, the one that explained once and for all why unmarried couples shouldn't live together—and how she'd ended up making love with Riley was beyond Adrienne.

Beyond the closed bathroom door, she heard him moving around. It wasn't hard to hear him. Riley getting ready for work was no noisier than a herd of elephants. Trying to hurry, mentally chanting prayers that her stomach would stop pitching acid, she climbed into her clothes and then reached for the tubes of war paint in the medicine cabinet.

She had one eye subtly brushed with a layer of mascara when the chants stopped working. The uncontrollable wave of nausea hit her as fast as a summer storm. She barely had time to lean over the sink—and at the same time, she could hear Riley whistling in the hall.

Riley didn't whistle in the morning; he snapped and growled. Furthermore, their mutual world was falling apart and he was walking around out there as blithe as a bumblebee. Could he have forgotten she was pregnant? Blocked the trauma from his mind? Had he totally flipped out? And she'd woken up dominantly aware that he had not mentioned marriage the night before. She'd have argued with him if he had. She'd have fought him if he had. But still, Riley had some hopelessly archaic ideas about honor and women, and she'd been so sure...

At the moment, she felt sure of nothing. She managed to run the water taps on full to cover the sound of her being sick, then groped for the cleanser to cover her tracks. After that all she could do was lean against the porcelain, weak and shivering. Unfortunately the pitiful whistling rendition of ''Rag Town'' ceased just outside the door. He rapped once.

''You okay in there, brown eyes?''

''Just fine,'' she sang out.

''You're not sick or anything, are you?''

''Heavens, no! I'm just fin—'' Too late she saw the knob turning.

Riley peered in, took one look at her and shook his head. ''So...we're not feeling so chipper this morning?''

She felt like last year's leftovers. "Riley, please go away."

"Okay," he said cheerfully, but he didn't. In one fell swoop, he had her sitting on the toilet seat and was running warm water on a washcloth to wash her face. She didn't want her face washed. She wanted to curl up somewhere in the fetal position with a blanket over her head. "This is why you've been spending so much time in the bathroom these past mornings, isn't it?"

"No," she denied.

"Yes, it is." Riley mopped her face, then ran cold water and squeezed a layer of toothpaste on her brush as if he thought she'd totally lost the capacity to do it herself. "Naturally you're staying home today."

"I'm not staying home, there's no reason to. The whole thing goes away as fast as it comes."

"Does it?" he asked interestedly.

She simply couldn't sit there and discuss morning sickness with Riley. Looking at him was tough enough. He must have showered before she did because his hair was still damp at the edges, coal dust with a sheen. His gray suit always made his shoulders look like a linebacker's. His face had clean, strong, angular lines, not a boy's features but a man's, and there wasn't a woman this side of the Atlantic who wouldn't look at Riley twice. He was good-looking. He was sexy. He had eyes that could strip a woman in three seconds flat and a natural virility that made a woman's nerves tingle.

She had to look like she felt. A woman who had just thrown up. The way Riley's eyes rested on her, you would think she was the last brownie in the pan, and his inexplicable cheerfulness seemed additional proof that he had a seriously unhinged mind this morning. In fact, she was concerned enough about his behavior to test it. "Did you remember that we have a dinner with your boss Thursday night?"

"Hmmm?"

"You have to go."

"So we'll go. That's Thursday and this is now. You put your face on and I'll fix breakfast, some nice bacon and eggs—" he glanced at her face "—some nice soda crackers and tea."

Adrienne stared after him. He'd been grousing about the dinner with his boss for weeks. Riley usually rated business dinners lower than snake bites, but now he was whistling again.

Ten minutes later, Adrienne appeared at the breakfast table. He'd put out a fork and knife to go with a small plate of soda crackers. She had the brief inclination to hold her head in her hands. "Riley?"

"Hmmm?"

One of them had to behave rationally. It was obvious to Adrienne that she was the only volunteer. "I'm not keeping the baby," she said quietly.

"No?"

"No." She finished the four crackers he'd arranged on the plate and stood to reach into the cupboard for the package. The whole package. Riley's sudden smile was unnerving when she sat down—he just didn't seem to realize how terribly serious a subject this was. "You know my mother and grandmother— nurturing women don't exactly run in my family, and

I haven't one reason to think I'd be any different. I faced a long time ago that I wasn't maternal material.''

Riley, noting her polishing off the crackers, slid half of his scrambled eggs on her plate.

''Are you listening to me?'' she asked fiercely.

''To every word,'' he assured her.

''Maybe I never planned a pregnancy but that doesn't mean I don't care. If I'm stuck having this baby, I'm sure as brass going to make sure it ends up with a mother who knows what she's doing and would do everything right. A child belongs around a mother who—'' she hesitated ''—can make chocolate-chip cookies.'' Her eyes searched his. ''We both know I can't boil water.''

''You're exaggerating. You do a beautiful job of boiling water. It's just when you try to do something tricky like opening a soup can that you—''

''Riley, this is not time to tease.'' She dived into the scrambled eggs. ''The only diaper I've ever seen was in an ad on TV. I've already had two horrible nightmares about diaper pins—dammit, don't smile. I'm telling you they were *nightmares*.''

He wiped the smile off his face and said soberly, ''You should have woken me up if you were having bad dreams.''

She waved the sidetrack comment aside. ''There's nothing wrong with working moms, but if I had my choice, I'd want the child around a mother who'd be there when he got home from school. Who was good at patching skinned knees, who always had time to read, and listen, and be there. A good mother creates a whole nurturing atmosphere.'' She lifted a hand in a helpless gesture. ''I spend all day, every day, surrounded by people who are doing their best to tear their lives apart—that's the kind of atmosphere that I know. You think I'd risk bringing that home to a child?''

Riley's first impulse was to tease her silly for worry about such crazy, irrelevant nonsense. Parents learned to diaper babies; a child's whole future was hardly dependent on homemade chocolate-chip cookies; and she had as much in common with her mother as 14-carat gold did with the rings that came out of a Cracker Jacks box.

His impulse to tease her died a quick death when he realized she was serious. His intelligent Adrienne was actually afraid of a diaper. His perceptive courtroom counselor had no concept of her own giving and loving instincts, and his strong, self-reliant lover was worried sick about things he'd never conceived she'd be worried about.

Since she'd finished the crackers and most of his eggs, he forked two slices of bacon onto her plate. He didn't know what else to do.

''So having the baby adopted is the best possible answer,'' she finished finally.

''If that's what you want.''

Adrienne saw him glance abruptly at his watch and frown. Lurching to his feet, he carted plates to the sink. He always had to leave ten minutes before she did. She trailed him as far as the hall. ''You understand? Why adoption is the best option for the baby?''

"I understand why you feel it is." He buttoned his suit jacket and reached for his briefcase.

She automatically straightened his tie. "So if we agree on adoption, the rest of the solutions fall into place. I move out. A little more than seven months from now, I have the baby. In the interim, I have fifty states to find the absolutely perfect couple to adopt the child. In that way, the baby can have the best possible home and—"

"Adrienne."

Most mornings, Riley was pliable. Most mornings he was awake enough to respond to an air raid. When he nudged up her chin with his thumb, Adrienne was again aware that he just wasn't himself. His hand gently cupped her cheek, but his eyes were intensely blue, bold and battle bright.

"You were so sure I was going to argue with you last night," he murmured, "and I think you woke up even more sure I was going to argue with you this morning. Only that's not going to happen, love. We're going to deal with this your way—totally and completely—with only one teensy exception. You are not moving out."

"Riley—"

"You try it and I'll find you. You try moving into a cave and I'll find that cave. You are not going to be alone and pregnant, so wipe that thought permanently out of your mind." His tone was rock hard one instant, soothing and easy the next. "And now we have that clear, give us a kiss, because I'm sure as hell not going to be able to make it through the day without one."

She didn't give him a kiss. He took one. Just one, in which her sanity hovered somewhere between the crush of his mouth and the overwhelming warmth of his body. He tasted like coffee and peppermint toothpaste. He smelled like clean soap and lime. And he felt like the man she had hopelessly, desperately fallen in love with.

When he closed the door, though, she felt despair. Maybe she'd been crazy to think Riley would walk out on her, but staying together was equally impossible. He didn't understand. Everything had changed.

A treasured, well-savored memory popped into her mind that underlined her low mood. When was it, weeks back? She'd been soaking in a hot tub after a perfectly rotten day. Riley had shown up naked in the doorway, shut off all the lights, brought in a candle and two glasses of champagne and slid into the tub with her.

What happened after that was typical of her impulsive, wildly romantic Riley...but what would happen if he tried that now was the point. For openers, she'd have to turn down the alcohol because of the doctor's orders. Even assuming she ignored the doctor's orders, the first sip of champagne would undoubtedly make her throw up. And weeks down the pike, even a dark candlelit room wouldn't conceal a most unromantic, burgeoning tummy.

She wasn't going to stick around and see it happen—patience instead of passion in his eyes. Riley's natural impulsiveness squelched under forced responsibilities he'd never asked for. He was the only man with whom she'd ever come close to feeling secure, not just in bed but in living and caring and sharing every day with him. That security, though, came from knowing their relationship was based on an equal exchange of needs.

Nothing was equal now. What they had was unforgettably special, but Adrienne had always known that the best of relationships deteriorated when either partner was tied down or cornered.

She'd a thousand times rather call it off now than let that happen, and as far as this baby... unconsciously Adrienne's palm slipped down to her abdomen. Except for the smallest protrusion, there was nothing there, nothing she could feel to explain this terrible anxiety and panic.

It's obvious why you feel it—you don't want the baby in any way, she told herself fiercely, frowned, and abruptly raced for the kitchen.

The morning had been so traumatic that she'd nearly forgotten to take the baby's vitamin that Liz had prescribed.

Chapter Three

Riley canceled a lunch meeting and picked up some fast food en route to the bookstore. Inside, the clerk frowned at the sight of his paper-wrapped hamburger. He shot her a wink and a smile, and the next thing he knew he had more help than he could handle.

The teenage clerk was very sweet, very young and very crush-prone. It took all his tact to convince her that he didn't need any help, which as it happened, was a lie. Another woman wandered into his aisle and plucked a book off the shelf faster than the snap of a finger. How the hell did she find it so easy?

There seemed to be more than a hundred books to choose from, starting with Spock and ending with space-age concepts of parenting. There was a *Mother's Almanac*, a *Father's Almanac*, books on pregnancy, books on child raising, books on how to increase the intelligence of a fetus in the womb, books on discipline, books on childbirth underwater, books on...

In the end, he scooped up everything he could carry. The clerk's eyes widened at the size of the stack on the counter. "I take it you're gonna be a father?"

"Yes." The moment she started punching buttons, he knew he wasn't carrying enough cash.

"First-time dad?"

"Yes." He flipped through his wallet for a gold card.

"Do you care whether it's a boy or a girl?"

"No." Actually he cared about Adrienne, which was why he was buying the books. She was so shook. So shook, so worried, so scared, and so sure the whole world had turned upside down—and maybe it had. All Riley knew was that for the past twenty-four hours he felt as if he'd fallen into a bowl with a food mixer on high speed. Adrienne's mind was on babies; his was on her. Maybe the books held no answers, but they were a start to understanding what she was feeling.

With his gold card retrieved, he reached for the book sack—which seemed to weigh between a ton and a ton and a half—and used his shoulder to open the store door. An April breeze whipped through his hair, the wind crackling through the new spring leaves like rustling taffeta. Halfway to his car, it hit him with all the surprise of the first bomb of Pearl Harbor.

He was going to be a father. Him. Riley Stuart. A father.

He had been whistling that morning for just that reason, of course, but then the connection had only been a vague emotion. A family and children had always been an equally vague plan in his mind—sometime, after he finished law school. Sometime, after he got himself established. Sometime, after he had a job that required no traveling.

Sometime had just arrived, and with it a slow

thrumming beat in the middle of his chest. He wanted it. He wanted the child, suddenly and fiercely and totally. Adrienne's daughter, with her pride and sassiness and soft vulnerable eyes. Or a son, with her smarts and his shoulders—he'd die if a daughter got his shoulders. If it were a daughter, she'd have to go in a convent before she was ten if she looked like Adrienne. But his son...his son could go to Dartmouth.

An old man bumped into him, glared and mumbled past with some comment about people blocking sidewalks.

Riley's step picked up, but his focus was blind. Always, there had been a woman in those "sometime" fantasies. Not just *a* woman. *The* woman: lover, mate, wife, friend. From the day he met her, Adrienne fit all the niches but one.

Numbers were particularly relevant because a family started at three. Something was wrong in the scenario of just father and son, or just father and daughter. The snapshot without Adrienne didn't work. Life without Adrienne didn't work. Convincing her of that was obviously going to be tricky, particularly since he didn't dare mention marriage.

And he had no idea where he was going to hide all the books.

For the first time in weeks Adrienne felt like herself. She'd won her case in court, nausea hadn't plagued her all day and she had energy and good humor to burn. Humming something catchy, she pulled the emerald-green dress over her head and reached back for the zipper. Nothing ever went wrong when she wore the green dress. Maybe it wasn't new, but it had always been as lucky as a rabbit's foot for her.

She zipped it past her hips, then frowned. The zipper didn't want to squeeze any farther. Her tummy seemed to have popped out three inches in the past twenty-four hours. She hesitated, then took it off and reached for the jeweled print chemise in the closet. All right, so she couldn't wear her favorite. Who needed a rabbit's foot, anyway? Absolutely nothing was going to spoil her mood tonight.

"I hate going to these things."

Adrienne stepped out of the closet, and noted with amusement that Riley's scowl was as dark as a thundercloud. "I know you do," she said soothingly.

"There's no reason to go. I'll just call Brown and tell him we both caught the bubonic plague."

Smothering a chuckle, she watched him jerk a tie around his neck as though he intended to strangle himself. Riley in a temper had a lot in common with a baby in his "Terrible Twos." Serene and calm, she walked over to button his shirt cuffs. "You make this huge fuss every time, and all for nothing. You always end up having a great time and even if you didn't, it's only for a few short hours—"

"*Wasted* hours. Listening to Brown rant on about his right-wing policies. And his wife's as charming as a barracuda. She'll probably feed us raw fish. She did last time."

"Riley, this is your boss's way of telling you you're doing a great job."

"Yeah? He wants to do that, he can give me a raise."

"He gave you a raise. In fact, he gave you two this past year." Adrienne patiently removed the gold-and-green tie and replaced it with a blue-and-gold one. He was wearing a blue suit—her choice. If she'd left it to Riley, he'd be wearing a hair shirt and sackcloth. "He's vetting you for the head of the industrial relations department. You know that."

"He's not *vetting* me. He's pushing me toward it."

"He knows you're considering hanging out your own shingle. You can't crucify Brown for offering you every possible nugget to make you stay—it's your own fault he thinks you're irreplaceable—and tonight is hardly as complicated as all that. I don't know why you let yourself get so worked up over one dinner, one evening." She finished tying his tie and patted it down. Mad or not, he looked wonderful. Virile and vital and blue-eyed—but regretfully, stubborn.

"We're not going," he said flatly.

"Okay," she agreed, all soothing smiles, and then did what any other red-blooded woman would do—dragged him to the car.

An hour later, they drove past the wrought-iron gates into Andrew Brown's estate. The three-story sprawling mansion was built of white stone, its elegance suiting the life-style of a man who owned an international manufacturing company with subsidiaries all over the world. Brown had a full staff of attorneys whose specialties ranged from corporate law to industrial relations. Riley was the lawyer Brown called in the middle of the night to settle a labor problem in Germany. Or in Japan. Or in Topeka, Kansas.

Riley might have dreams of starting his own practice, but as Adrienne knew well, the corporate life hadn't hurt him. Riley adored those labor disputes; the tougher the better. As she also knew, once she got him inside he would not only behave nicely but shine in the crowd. He always did. The only trick was getting him inside.

"We could still back out," Riley muttered as he escorted Adrienne to the door. "Brown would never know we were here. I didn't see anything wrong with the bubonic plague excuse."

If he were a two-year-old, she would have stood him in a corner. Since he was a grown man, she swung her arms around his neck and kissed his mouth. There was lovemaking and then there was sex. There were occasions when nothing worked as well as plain old sex on Riley. His prickly mood dissolved the minute he felt the snuggle of her body, the deliberate rub of her lips. They both knew she was manipulating him. They both liked it. "You're not only going in there. You're going to have a good time," she informed him.

He considered that while he took another kiss. "I'd rather go parking." He wanted more than another kiss. When he nuzzled her throat, he discovered she'd chosen a wicked scent tonight. Deliberately. "When's

the last time you were made love to in the back seat
of a car?''

"Never."

"Never?" He lifted his head and most leisurely
surveyed her mouth, her throat, her eyes. He looked
until a streak of coral climbed her cheeks, delighting
him. "We're going to have an awfully good time,
taking care of that serious lack in your education—"

"Riley!" She rang the bell, her nerves tingling. He
did it to her all the time. Made her feel desired and
special. Made her feel like no one mattered but the
two of them, that they could conquer anything as long
as they were together. That's always how it had been
with them, at least until she discovered the pregnancy...but quickly, quickly she banished the pregnancy from her mind. Not tonight. She was in such a
radiant mood that nothing could disturb it.

Her mood dipped just a hair when their hostess
answered the door. If Maud fit the stereotype of her
name, she'd be staid and proper. Instead Brown's second wife had a long white throat uniquely suited to
the wearing of diamonds, a smooth coil of Egyptian-
dark hair, and a shrewd eye for an up-and-coming
man—particularly if he was a looker. She smiled a
lambent welcome at Adrienne, but made a point of
bussing Riley before ushering them both through the
marble foyer.

"What's new in divorce settlements, Adrienne?"
Maud asked, although her attention still focused on
Riley as she led them toward the intimate—a mere

twenty—dinner party. "You and I never seem to have the chance to just sit down and talk."

"Maybe tonight," Adrienne murmured, annoyed that she felt unsettled instead of amused. Maud's antics had always been a source of humor, not stress. If Maud hadn't made a token play for Riley, Adrienne would have had the kindness to immediately call the paramedics, knowing the older woman was ill. Maud was just...Maud.

Typically, when Riley freed his arm, Maud made certain her breast brushed his wrist. Just as typically, Riley shot Adrienne a comical look. Any other night she would have chuckled with him, but somehow her mood had shifted another tiny hair. Riley could handle himself around far more skilled barracudas than his boss's wife. It was just...

Just nothing, you goose. Within minutes of entering the living room, she automatically deserted Riley and did what she did best: worked the room. Riley wouldn't care if she curled on a couch with her shoes off, but Adrienne did—he hadn't quit Brown's yet, and until he was certain of that decision, she had a job to do. She listened to Andrew Brown's political monologue, circulated around the corporate heads and made careful small talk with the wives.

It wasn't Adrienne's favorite kind of evening, but she'd walked in confidently prepared to enjoy it. There was just no reason for the inexplicable sensation of isolation that kept creeping up on her. The Browns always invited a similar group. Ambition dominated the ambience, and an itty bit of back stabbing and in jokes dominated the conversations, but those dynamics came with the corporate world. Adrienne knew the game and was more than willing to play it for Riley. He was hardheaded about honesty; it didn't hurt to be nice. Most of the men in the room had wives to play diplomat, but Riley...

Didn't have a wife.

She shook off the word "wife" and plastered a radiant smile back on her face. Maud found her just before dinner. "For a change I put you on the other side of the table from Riley, darling. Dinner conversation's so boring when we stick couples together, don't you think?"

Adrienne mentally released a humorous sigh. Maud tried her best to stir things up at a party, so it was no surprise to see that her hostess had settled Riley between two women—the only other two women at the party who were single.

As she eyed his companions across the table, she thought wickedly that the two ladies were in for a treat. The tall, quiet blonde had looked desperately nervous when she first walked in; the younger brunette had painfully shy dark eyes. Neither, clearly, had expected to walk into the fiercely competitive atmosphere of Maud's "little" dinner. Riley, of course, would have them at ease before either knew what hit them.

Adrienne had known from the day she met him that Riley attracted women and also that he loved to flirt. She'd never called him on it, because there was no point. He hadn't gone blind the day he met her. He liked women, always had and always would—and what was the harm? You can't hold a man with jealousy or by misunderstanding every casual conversation he had with another woman. If a woman was going to hold a man, it had to be with what they had together.

The dining room was a massive business in mahogany and gold. Candles winked from sterling holders and silverware clinked for the opening course of vichyssoise. Adrienne took one look at the potato soup, felt her stomach warningly pucker and glanced again across the table.

The gentle-eyed brunette was smiling now. Adrienne hadn't noticed before that she had on a formfitting white knit dress...and a stomach as flat as a pancake. So did the tall, quiet blonde, who suddenly wasn't so quiet. Riley had said something to make her laugh. Nervousness forgotten, the blonde's face took on animation and life—she was really very attractive, with intelligent, bright eyes and a natural warmth in her laughter. Adrienne was sure she would like her. Riley had never gone for airheads. He did like a lithe, long figure, a woman in control of her life, a woman...who wasn't pregnant.

Someone passed a plate of asparagus in front of her. Riley caught her eye over the table and winked. It was a sexy wink, an intimate wink, a private message passed just between the two of them. *We'll be out of here soon,* his blue eyes promised her.

Not soon enough. To Adrienne's utter horror, a

lump filled her throat too thick to swallow and a wave
of unmanageable emotion started to engulf her.

"Would you excuse me a moment?" she murmured to the man next to her and slipped away from
the table. Although it couldn't be ten feet to the doorway, the distance seemed like ten miles, and once out
in the hall, she had no memory of where the powder
room was.

By the time she found the almond-and-gold powder
room, she had a direct problem with a flood—pouring
uncontrollably out of her eyes. *Good grief, what is
the matter with you?* Too shivery to stand, she
dropped to the edge of the almond tub. The whole
thing was crazy. Huge, crazy hiccuping sobs kept
emerging from her lungs and wouldn't stop. Tears
streamed from her eyes like an unplugged dike. She
mentally called herself a hundred names, but it didn't
help.

Someone knocked on the door. Mortified, she
gulped back a new flush of tears and called out, "Be
out in a minute!"

"Adrienne, open the door."

As fast as she recognized Riley's voice, she
reached for one of her hostess's impeccable guest
towels and doused it with cold water.

"My boss is going to be irritated with me if I break
down his door, love. It would be a lot easier if you'd
just unlock it."

"Can't." She was positive her voice sounded normal, yet his response was immediate.

"I really will break it down, honey."

He wouldn't, she promised herself, but there was a brief second when she wasn't absolutely sure. Plastering the towel over her eyes, she jerked the lock and the door. "I just got a little something in my eye," she said blithely. "It's all taken care of. For heaven's sake, go back to the dinner party!"

Riley closed and latched the door behind him. The spacious powder room abruptly became crowded, particularly when he loomed close enough to peek around the corner of the towel. He didn't need more than one quick look at her eyes. "All taken care of, hmm?"

If he'd just sounded appalled or impatient, she could have pulled herself together. Instead he sounded so damned *dear*. Her lungs heaved out a horrible sound and the tears started pouring again. "I'm sorry. I don't know what's wrong with me. This is so stupid!"

"It's okay."

"It's not okay. It's disgusting. Nobody killed my dog. Nobody started a world war. Nobody hurt me. I was just sitting there and everything was fine——"

"Adrienne, it's okay. It's perfectly normal. There's a whole section on blues starting on page 78 of the pregnancy manual." He plunked down onto the toilet seat and pulled her on his lap, jamming her cheek to his shirt and wrapping his arms around her.

"What blues? What pregnancy manual?"

"Shh." He rocked her. She was shaking so hard, crying so hard, that for a while he couldn't do anything else. He heard something about a green dress that didn't fit, some woman's flat, flat stomach, and that he had every right and freedom to talk to a beautiful blonde.

She lifted her head to repeat fiercely, "Every right, Riley." He jammed her cheek back to his chest. In good time the tears finally slowed, even hurricanes had to quit sometime. He patted his pocket for a handkerchief before he remembered that he had never in his life carried a handkerchief. The Browns had several thousand dollars' worth of brass fixtures, recessed lighting, marble and fancy towels, but no tissues. He unraveled some toilet paper and made her blow her nose.

"I just can't believe I'm doing this. It's so stupid!"

"It's not stupid."

"It is, too! I've never been moody or overemotional in my entire life!"

"You were never pregnant before in your entire life." He smoothed back her hair. She really was a mess. He couldn't recall ever seeing Adrienne such a total disaster before. Her nose was red, so were her eyes; her cheeks were blotchy and her hair, well, he'd messed up her hair. Dammit, he loved her!

"You have to go back to the party."

He expressed his feelings about the party in a simple four-letter word.

"Riley! This business dinner is part of your work. There's no way I'm going to let me—or this pregnancy—interfere with your job. That's the exact reason I told you that we'd both be better off if I looked for another place and moved out."

"Then you could have the blues all by yourself?"

"What is this 'blues' business? I don't have any blues; I just went temporarily bananas. And you don't have to be nice when someone behaves like a total fruitcake."

"The blonde is a no one, honey. Just someone sitting next to me. I was just talking to her."

"You're welcome to talk to her."

"I can see that."

"She was beautiful—"

"Heavy mascara. Bad teeth. Hips like an army tank," he improvised rapidly.

"She looked so smart."

"She had the IQ of a frog."

"She did not. She looked smart. And not only smart, she looked nice."

Three of the pregnancy manuals had sections on blues. None of them exactly equipped Riley to handle this. Adrienne was the most sensible, practical woman he knew. Until now. And until now, she'd never had a jealous bone in her body. "Okay, she was nice. But she wasn't you, love."

"Me? You *have* to get it through your head, Riley. You like svelte and slim. I'm going to look like an elephant in another few months."

"I like elephants."

"Not ugly out-of-control elephants." From the deep blue—from absolutely nowhere—she suddenly whispered, "I'm so scared."

So he kissed her. And when her arms went up around his neck, he kissed her again.

By the time he kissed her a third time, the blood was humming through his veins and his heart was full. Her responsiveness had nothing to do with passion and—whether or not she knew it—everything to do with trust. For those few brief moments he had a taste of it all. The compelling power of loving her. The devastating weakness of knowing she loved him just as much, if she'd just give that trust a chance.

In due time, of course, it occurred to both of them that there was something less than romantic about necking on a toilet seat in his boss's house. Adrienne was the first one to start chuckling—an honest chuckle. She was back to herself again.

Riley left her to seek out Maud. When his boss's wife forgot to play vamp, she had a decent head on her shoulders. At the same time Maud made their excuse of sudden illness to the dinner party, Riley was sneaking Adrienne out the back door into a star-speckled April night.

The sneaking wasn't strictly necessary, but it was fun. Racing to the car made them feel like kids playing hooky, and Adrienne was breathless with laughter when she climbed in the passenger seat. If Riley had anything to say about it, it wasn't the last time she was going to laugh that evening. He wanted her to forget that upsetting bout of blues.

Even more than that, he wanted her to know that he'd be there for her—not just for the laughter, but the tough times as well.

April finished off cool, but the whole month of June had been hot and sweltering. As she walked into the apartment, Adrienne welcomed the flush of air conditioning with a heartfelt sigh. Pushing off her shoes and laying down her briefcase, she made a bee-line for the kitchen.

Riley had a late-afternoon meeting, which meant dinner would be late, which in any moral framework on earth justified an immediate snack. She bypassed the butter brickle ice cream, the Muenster cheese and the caramel corn, all of which appealed to her last week. This week it was spinach. Freshly washed and raw.

Until this pregnancy, there wasn't a soul in her life who could have accused Adrienne of greed. If Riley had been there, she'd have delicately plucked a leaf or two. Since he wasn't, she pulled the whole bag from the lower shelf of the refrigerator. Munching ravenously, she sorted through the mail, and when her snack was finished headed for the bedroom to change clothes.

She peeled off her work clothes and pulled on a pair of cotton pants, discovered they wouldn't zip—much less button—cast them off and tried another pair. Five minutes later, her entire summer wardrobe of slacks had been rejected—none of them fit—and she was fingering through Riley's closet, muttering about the weight-gaining potential of spinach.

She was tugging on one of his oldest, softest blue oxford shirts—Riley hadn't commented on her usurping his shirt wardrobe any more than he'd mentioned her recent love of spinach—when she noticed the stuffed animal.

It wasn't your usual small, cuddly teddy bear. It was a unicorn, white, soft-furred, and half as tall as she was. Although Riley had tucked it in the far corner beyond the aquariums, it wasn't the kind of thing one could miss for long.

Although she continued buttoning his shirt, she couldn't take her eyes off the toy. She had deliberately "missed" a great deal over the past few weeks. She hadn't noticed the *Father's Almanac* buried under Riley's *Wall Street Journal*, for example. She had also paid no attention to the pregnancy manual under the bathroom sink, with its earmarked pages and highlighted paragraphs.

Twenty-five pounds of white unicorn was tougher to ignore. The look of the toy made her feel as though a rug had been swept out from under her.

For the past two months, Adrienne had done the best she knew how to pretend the pregnancy didn't exist. Since the dinner party, she had temporarily, warily, dropped the idea of moving out. Riley simply became totally irrational on the subject. But she had only agreed to stay until the baby was born. And only, she promised herself, if she could make their relationship work as it always had.

For his sake, she hadn't mentioned babies. He'd caught on to her cravings, but she'd carefully hidden her queasy stomach and bouts of blues from him. A dozen times, she'd tactfully told him that he had the same freedom to leave he'd always had. If his life was negatively affected in any way by this pregnancy, she was prepared to pack her bags.

She'd worked hard to make sure nothing was changed for Riley. She was changed, though, and there was no fighting it. No matter how often she told herself she didn't want the baby, sometimes this elation would sweep through her...sometimes an extraordinary sensation of softness...and sometimes her crazy hormones had an embarrassing erotic and exotic effect when the lights went out. She couldn't seem to keep her hands off him, which thoroughly delighted Riley, the rogue.

The passion was real, the pretending becoming increasingly hard. She *was* pregnant. Their lives *had* changed. Decisions *had* to be made about the baby. Soon, those things had to be faced and dealt with. She'd already dealt with the reason he hadn't brought up marriage. *He never wanted a permanent relationship with you, Adrienne. You understood that from the very beginning.*

She couldn't understand his buying the unicorn at all.

The apartment door slammed. She was still sitting on the bed when Riley strode in. He was always a dynamo of energy after a desk-bound day. By the time he found her, he'd already peeled off his suit jacket and was tearing at his tie.

He took one look at her dressed in his shirt and pounced. You'd think he hadn't seen her in a week the way he kissed her. You'd think the man was magic the way she responded...and she did respond, eyes closed and blindly reaching for him. It was a foolish illusion in her head, she knew, yet Riley had the dreadful gift of making her feel cherished, wanted, needed.

He also wasn't happy until she was good and unraveled. Straightening with a merciless grin—a promise for later—he strode toward his closet. "You have to wait until after dinner."

"Do I smell the reek of egotism in this room?" she wondered aloud.

"You want me. Go ahead, admit it. I won't tell."

"You? Of the hairy chest and the bony knees?"

"You love my knees."

She did, it was true, but that was only because she was insane about the man, in bed and much more disastrously, out of it. Her mood dropped like a plummeting boulder, though, when her gaze darted back to the unicorn. "What are you doing, Riley?" she asked quietly.

"At this precise instant, stripping." He exhibited one hairy leg around the closet door as proof, then momentarily reemerged in cotton jeans. "It's one hot night out there."

"That's not what I meant. Who is that stuffed animal supposed to be for?"

He saw where she was focused. "The baby?" He tugged a T-shirt over his head. "I suppose you think it's a little big for a newborn."

"I think it would be a big toy for a baby cow," she said wryly. "Only we're not having a cow. We're having a baby that both of us have agreed would be best off given up for adoption.''

"I was fairly sure you hadn't changed your mind about that.''

"You know I haven't.''

He nodded. "I also know that your standards are pretty tough—some might say impossibly tough, since you've totally rejected every adoption agency you've talked to. So I've been doing a little research, and came up with someone to adopt the baby for you. Someone you know. Someone where you'd be able to keep track of what happened to the child, and someone where you can be positive the baby will be raised with values you value.''

For a moment air seemed locked in her lungs. None of the adoption agencies she'd talked to had offered those things. They'd told her she was making "impossible demands.'' One caseworker in Chicago had had the nerve to suggest that Adrienne did not sound emotionally sure she could give up the baby, which was totally untrue. She was relieved and reassured that Riley had found someone. It was just, momentarily, difficult to breathe.

"Who is this 'someone'?'' she asked hollowly.

He shot her a fast grin. "Me.''

"You?" But as fast as she lurched off the bed, Riley had ducked through the doorway and left the room.

Chapter Four

Adrienne bolted after him, and found him calmly reaching for a spoon in the kitchen drawer. "You can't possibly adopt the baby!"

"No? Why not?" He lifted the lid on the earthenware pot that had been simmering all day. Immediately the scents of orange peel and garlic and red wine spiced the air. His French *Boeuf en Daube*, an old favorite of Adrienne's, was done.

"For all the hundred obvious reasons starting with the most important one." Adrienne sank onto the kitchen chair as if it was the last seat on the bus. "You don't want the baby. If you'd wanted it, you'd have told me a long time before this."

He gently contradicted her. "Actually I always wanted a child or two, but the idea always went on the back burner—after law school, after establishing myself in a career, after I had a house." He carefully didn't mention marriage as part of those plans. He knew her reaction to the word too well. "I guess I always thought there's be an obvious 'ideal time' to be a father, but I'm thirty-five now. I don't want to be so gray haired and arthritic that I can't swing a bat in the yard with my kid."

"You never said any of that before," she said in a small voice.

Carrying the salad bowl to the sink, he fluffed her bangs. Poor baby, she looked so shell-shocked. She was also past four months pregnant, and time was running out. For the past few weeks Adrienne had taken up the nasty habit of catering to his every whim, laughing at his worst jokes, shielding him from every little stress. Little stresses like a pregnancy, for instance. She seemed determined to pretend the baby didn't exist. He'd tried it her way, but the days kept passing like a time bomb. He had to do something to get through that sweet thick head of hers that her lover was not deserting ship.

"I didn't talk about it before for a lot of reasons." He handed her the silverware to set the table. "I think both of us wanted some private time and space to adjust to the idea. And besides that, you've hardly invited any discussions about the baby."

"Because I didn't want you to feel obligated. I had no reason to think you wanted the child." Her voice caught on a reedy breath. "Riley, if I've been blind or insensitive about your feelings—"

He nipped that one fast. "Honey, you're sensitive to other people's feelings to a fault." Except her own, he thought fleetingly. "I never mentioned adopting the child, because when you first told me you were pregnant, I could see all the obvious obstacles. Sure, I can picture my carrying an urchin on my shoulders, but what do I know about chicken pox and colic? Then there's my job—working for Brown, I'm on the road too much. And I don't like the idea of raising a kid in an apartment. Then there's the whole thing of 'single dads.' There are lots of single moms out there, not half as many single dads, possibly because we're not half as good at the job.''

He watched her carefully set two knives around his plate, two forks around her own. Then she started folding napkins. Enough for a week.

"Anyway, as far as colic and chicken pox, I figure I could learn. And as far as being a good father, I figure I could work at it. Hard. The job—hell. It'd be a tough financial go for a while, but in the long run I always wanted to hang out my own shingle. And the apartment isn't any problem at all. You like it, sweet, and you also keep telling me that one of us has to move the minute the baby is born."

Her head shot up. "Babies don't belong with living-together couples, Riley. It's just not right."

"I totally agree. So you keep the place, and in the meantime I'll look for a house. Something small, with a little lawn and trees. You wouldn't object if I were the one to adopt the baby, would you?"

"I...no, of course not." She pleated another napkin. A cinema of snapshots flooded through her mind—Riley rocking a baby, carrying a little one on his shoulders to the zoo, playing Santa Claus. In every mental photo, the child looked deliriously happy, and why not? No one had more patience than Riley; he was affectionate and warm, perceptive and accepting—an absolute natural as a father. "I think it's a fine idea," she said brightly. "I just..."

"You just what, love?"

She just felt like someone had smashed her in the

teeth. He wanted the baby, but not her. If he'd wanted her, he would have brought up marriage. Okay, okay, possibly she'd reacted like a cat on a hot spit any time he'd even mentioned wedding rings in the past, but bigger truths dominated her mind now—the same bigger truths and insecurities that had haunted her since the start of this pregnancy.

From the very beginning, she had never expected the relationship to last; she had always expected him to leave her. The power of being in love had a lot in common with a newly opened champagne bottle. Nothing beat the fizz and the sparkle, but the bottle left open over time lost both. She'd seen it with her parents and she saw it every day in divorce court, but she'd always hoped—fiercely hoped—that it might take Riley just a little more time to realize he wasn't in love with her.

"What's wrong, honey?"

"Nothing," she said. He whisked the pile of napkins out of her hands, leaving her nothing to do. "I just don't know how a father goes about adopting his own baby."

"Neither do I. Pretty humorous, isn't it? Two attorneys in the same house and neither of us knows the laws affecting adoptions. Still, it'll be easy enough to find out...as long as you're sure you don't mind."

"Why on earth would I mind? It's your child."

"Yours, too," he reminded her casually. "So maybe you'd better be very sure of that, too, love."

"Sure of what?"

His gaze was as blue and intense as a hot summer sky. "That you don't want the child."

She suddenly blinked hard. Sometimes when she thought of the baby, this huge, wallowing sweet emotion engulfed her—she'd even dreamed of the three of them together, her holding the baby so tightly, Riley smiling, so happy, so proud. Maybe it was that picture of pride that made her wake up in the night, shivering all over, confused and upset and afraid.

It was so easy to hurt a child. She knew. There was no point in denying it; she came from a line of cold women. Her grandmother was as loving as a porcupine; her mother had been distant and insensitive. "A woman has to be tough to survive in this life," her mother always told her, but Adrienne hadn't been tough as a child. She'd been hurt, too easily and too often. Not anymore. As a grown woman, "You're just like me, darling" was her mother's favorite phrase.

Just like her. Adrienne couldn't seem to shake the phrase from her mind; it followed her as mercilessly as a shadow.

"Honey?"

She touched two fingers to her temples. "We've already discussed this. I want nothing to do with this baby. Nothing, Riley."

She knew she sounded coldhearted and insensitive. Hard. Like her mother. Which made it particularly difficult to understand why Riley brushed a soft, silent kiss on her brow as he set dinner in front of her.

He dropped the discussion, and she tried to put it out of her mind. It was one of those nights when Riley

had work after dinner and she didn't, so when he
holed up in the study, she fed the fish and did the
dishes, then sneaked a wash load of his shirts downstairs to the laundry. Riley's job was the wash, but
she knew he liked his shirts with a little starch and
he never took the time.

She checked on him later. From the spread of pa-
pers, she could see that he was three-quarters done,
so she brought him a weak whiskey—his way of
winding down—and turned on an extra light. Riley
would read in the dark if she let him. And outside,
the night had turned cool. She switched off the air
conditioning and threw open the windows, especially
in the bedroom. He didn't sleep well if it was stuffy,
and there was nothing stuffier than air conditioning.

"Adrienne!"

She pelted back to the study.

Black-rimmed glasses perched on his nose, he motioned to the place next to him on the couch. "Sit.
Before you wear yourself out."

"I wasn't worn out."

"Sit!"

"Wow," she murmured. "I'm real impressed. That
sounded like a dictatorial, chauvinistic order, and here
I thought you were such a cupcake."

Unfortunately he was within reaching distance of
her wrist, and Riley did like to wrestle. By the time
he'd tired of his acrobatics, she was lying on the
couch with her head in his lap, she was well kissed,
and his glasses were back on his nose.

Legal pad pages shifted past her. "Riley?"

"Hmm?"

"Your choosing to adopt the baby shouldn't have anything to do with our living together. They're two separate things. Nothing's changed. It's still not necessary to stay together because I'm pregnant. You have the same rights in the relationship you always had. If at any time the situation becomes awkward or you don't want to be here—"

"I know. I'm free to leave, which you tell me so often that my ego's beginning to feel like a chipped tooth," he said dryly. He closed the last law book and stacked it with the others. "Could you not try to kick me out of the house tonight? I'm too beat to pack."

She missed his small joke because she was so busy inhaling a lungful of air. "When we were talking before dinner...I know I must have sounded selfish and hard. Riley, I can't help it if I'm not maternal or nurturing."

"You just don't have a single caretaking instinct," he murmured helpfully.

"You know I don't." She tried to move, but his arm sliced off her attempt with a gentle stranglehold across her neck.

Riley would have loved to do more than strangle her. Earlier in the kitchen, he'd done what he set out to do—made sure she knew he wanted their child, and forced her to picture him in the role of father. When she hadn't rejected either idea, hope had sprung eternal. Maybe over time, if he were tiptoe careful,

he just might be able to sneakily bring up rings without her bolting for the door.

Eternal hope hadn't lasted long. It was going to be
damn tough to mention marriage when the pregnant
lady in question said flat-out she didn't want the baby.
His baby. He had wanted to hang up on that bruising
hurt, and he probably would have—if Adrienne
hadn't been the one with the bruised, panicked eyes
and skin as pale as parchment.

And she was still jumpy. Still pale.

"Is there some reason," Adrienne asked delicately,
"that you have your arm locked around my neck so
I can't move?"

"Yeah." He dropped the legal pad and pencil on
the lamp table. "You were about to jump up and pour
me another whiskey. I don't need one—nor did I ever
want or expect you to wait on me."

"I was never waiting on you!"

"I know," he said mildly. "You have no nurturing
instincts whatsoever. Lightning would probably strike
if you got the insane idea that you take care of everyone around you."

She knew he was teasing her, but she couldn't
smile because of the huge lump in her throat. It wasn't
easy to say what she wanted to say. "I just don't want
you to hate me because I don't want the baby."

"Sweetheart, there isn't a chance in this life I could
hate you. And whether or not you want the baby has
nothing to do with that."

"I don't want it, Riley."

"It's okay."

"At all."

"It's okay."

She woke in the middle of the night with the strangest sensation in her abdomen. Lying on her side, Riley was curled against her spine. They always slept that way, her back spooned to his chest, the front of his thigh nuzzled against the back of hers. Nothing was wrong this night, nothing different...except for that tiny, vague feeling.

Blinking in the dark, she waited, disoriented and sleepy. It happened again. Not pain. Just the brush of a velvet flutter from deep inside her.

"Riley!"

She turned over and grabbed him. He didn't move. A siren next to his ear wasn't likely to arouse Riley from a sound sleep. She had to shake his shoulders hard, and even then he didn't open his eyes. "If there's a burglar, you handle it," he mumbled groggily.

"Dammit, would you wake up? This is serious."

She grabbed his hand and locked it over her abdomen in the darkness. Nothing happened. Seconds ticked past, then minutes. Still, the flutter movement didn't repeat itself.

"This has a lot in common with someone waiting for tax reform." Riley yawned. "If you're sick, love, tell me. If you're in trouble, tell me. If not, I'm going back to sleep."

"Please, Riley!"

It happened again. Nothing monumental, nothing

huge. It simply felt the wings of a butterfly stirring inside her. "Did you feel it?" she yelped.

"No."

"It's real."

"What's real?"

"The baby!"

Although the aquarium lights were turned off, a full moon shimmered silvery light from the window. She saw him when he lifted up on one elbow and slowly skimmed his palm from her abdomen to her hip. "Not that you care about the baby," he said gravely.

She backpedaled like no one's business. "I never said I cared about the baby. It was just…you obviously do. Since you want to adopt it. So I thought you should know."

"Ah."

There was a definite smile on his face. A smug smile. An all-knowing male smile. Maybe that was why she kissed him—to wipe it off. Maybe she kissed him to divert him from traumatic deep-water subjects—like babies. Maybe she kissed him because she was sick of his being patient and accepting and kind when she knew darn well she'd been a pill to live with for weeks.

He didn't kiss back like he was all that annoyed either by babies or her.

For Adrienne, the future still loomed like an abyss. To bog Riley down because of her problems, though, was never what she'd wanted. The future was just going to have to wait.

Ruthlessly she pulled the pillow from behind his

head and let it drop on the floor. With the chilling determination of a hunter, she cornered her prey by climbing on top of him and anchoring his head still between her palms. She nipped his shoulder hard, to show him who was boss, and she kissed his lips very softly, to show him how much trouble he was in.

Riley would undoubtedly look more threatened if he weren't chuckling so hard.

"All right for you. Put your hands above your head," she ordered mercilessly.

"Oh, God. Is this going to be one of those impossible choices about my virtue or my life?"

"This is one of those times when you have to take your medicine like a man. Try and be brave. Fight me and I warn you, I won't be responsible."

He didn't try to fight her, but it was tough to pull off the role of aggressive seductress when your lover was choking back laughter. A tickle put him in his place, but unfortunately Riley wasn't a gentleman. He retaliated.

Later, she remembered a splash of covers and a tangle of limbs, giggling and being out of breath and Riley leaning over her with laughter in his eyes. That laughter softened, muted, darkened. And then his lips found hers.

His skin was stroking warm and his taste alluring. She knew what he wanted and she knew what he loved. The night blurred into sensations—hunger and softness, quicksilver kisses and Riley's eyes, so full of need, so full of want.

There was the briefest moment when she felt his

lips on her abdomen, a reminder of the baby that should have broken her mood, yet it didn't. The wonder of life inside her had started with Riley, and this night was about that kind of love. Wonder, precious and fragile, seeped into her senses, instilled her hands with feminine magic, filled her heart.

She pulled him down and took him in, a hundred times more wild than she knew herself to be, yet not so much with passion as tenderness. He was everything. She wanted him to know that, and in the darkness she gave him everything she was. With Riley, she had never had any other choice. With Riley, she had never wanted one.

Seven o'clock in the morning was no time to match socks. Riley scooped up the whole drawerful and tossed them in the open suitcase on his bed, his mood as pleasant as an irritated rattlesnake's.

He reached in the closet for a couple of white shirts and jammed them in on top of the socks. Adrienne was up and due out of the shower any minute. Like him, she'd been wakened by the telephone at six o'clock in the morning. It was his boss. There was union trouble in the West German plant. Riley's flight left in three hours. He had to hit the office first, and how was he supposed to remember where his passport was this early in the morning?

More relevant, he didn't want to leave. A year ago, he'd have jumped for the challenge of a European labor problem—dammit, they were fun—but a year ago Adrienne hadn't been pregnant.

The last place he wanted to be was five thousand miles away from her, and especially now. He knew she felt conflicting emotions about the baby, but last night she'd shown him what mattered. She wanted it. Desperately. He'd never seen her so hushed, so excited, so beautiful...or so suddenly scared as when she'd felt the baby's first movement.

He's guessed for a long time that her feelings about both the baby and marriage were mixed with fear. He understood her fear of marriage, but not her fear of the child. Adrienne could cope with corporate politics, a burned fuse, or survival in a blizzard, so nothing explained her irrational confusion over the baby except fear. Only one emotion excised common sense, overruled the brain, snaked up on you and locked its fangs where you were most vulnerable. Maybe Riley didn't understand why, but he sure as hell knew Adrienne was scared.

She hadn't been scared last night, and the memory still had him feeling dipped in honey. Hot? Her mouth alone could have caused a conflagration. Sensual? She had a tongue that ought to be licensed. And as far as love, Adrienne had redefined the word for him last night. She'd come to him with honesty and vulnerability, naked like he'd never seen her naked, and open from the soul.

He was going to marry that damn woman, and while one night didn't change the world, last night had surely made a difference. She trusted him. How could she have made love with him like that if she didn't? He'd be infinitely careful with her this morning, infinitely patient. She would undoubtedly be feeling sensitive this morning.

"Riley, I swear I could smack you. Get away from there!"

His head jerked up from the suitcase. "What's the matter?"

"You're going to get there with your shirts looking like accordions, and what are all these socks?" Adrienne bent over the case and dumped everything he'd packed. "Men! And you're not taking the gray suit. It has a spot. You're taking the blue one."

"Yes, ma'am."

"Don't touch those shirts!"

"Yes, ma'am." For that second "Yes, ma'am," she delivered the smack she'd been swearing about. Being Adrienne, the smack wasn't a hit but a kiss— and not at all the kind of kiss he'd counted on this morning. "Did you get your passport out of the top right-hand drawer of the desk in the den?"

"I was just going to do that," he said virtuously.

"I'll do it. I wouldn't trust you to find your own feet this early in the morning. You—" her finger wagged at him like a teacher's ruler "—get yourself a cup of coffee and stay out of my way."

Riley obediently poured himself a cup of coffee, brought it back to the bedroom, and stayed out of her way. For the next ten minutes he couldn't keep the grin off his face. There was no point in telling her he was a grown man, fully capable of packing his own suitcase. Adrienne took care of her clients like a lioness with threatened cubs; nothing was going to stop

her from taking care of her mother; and there was no
way he could entirely escape her protective instincts.
She flew between closet, dresser and suitcase faster
than a cyclone.

It took him a full ten minutes to realize she was
flying a bit too fast, teasing a little too hard. He knew
she was feeling well—the color in her cheeks was a
giveaway—but she was working as hard as a banshee
to avoid directly meeting his eyes. "Okay," he said
gently. "What's wrong?"

"Wrong? Nothing's wrong, except that I can't find
your red-and-blue tie."

"Forget the tie. What's bothering you?"

"Nothing!" She snapped the suitcase closed. Eyes
still averted from him, she grumbled, "If you're going to comment, though, I'd appreciate it if you'd just
get it over with."

A grown man developed instincts about when he'd
failed to notice something. Riley sensed all the feminine radar, but he'd be darned if he could make a
connection. Like a lost soul searching a map, he
checked her head to toe. She was wearing sort of a
classic-styled loose cream dress, low cream heels,
gold buttons in her ears and what appeared to be an
African scarf at her throat. "Ah, new earrings," he
said heartily.

"Cut it out, Riley."

"The scarf—"

"You gave me the scarf."

"And it looks great with the—" he thought fast
"—new dress."

The newness of the dress wasn't the problem. He knew from her too-bright laugh that it wasn't the problem, and Riley felt a slice of panic. None of the pregnancy manuals had this particular test, and it was obviously a critical one.

"Pretty funny looking, hmm? You would have really laughed if you'd seen me shopping. All the other maternity dresses had little sashes in back or bibs in front—you'd think all pregnant women wanted to regress to looking like Little Orphan Annie. I'm afraid I'm into elastic waists for the count, Riley. No more slim, no more svelte. I thought I could postpone it a little longer, but there's just nothing in the closet that fits anymore."

For a moment he was tempted to wave a hand in front of her eyes, just to make sure someone was home. Adrienne, vain? The same lady who blithely vacuumed in his oldest T-shirt?

But when he touched her soft cheek, he saw the fragility in her expression. This wasn't about her looks. It was about his reaction to her looks. "You thought I'd care, did you? No more slim, no more svelte? You thought I'd care?"

"Maybe not consciously."

"I have to be the one to tell you this, love," he said slowly, "But you have become more beautiful, not less, in the past few months. That goes for the skin, the eyes, the smile, and most definitely the little growing package in front. How could you doubt it?"

The tension faded from her expression, yet still she

said, "My mother said I looked like a toothpick carrying a watermelon."

Riley's eyes narrowed. "How did your mother get into this?"

"She went with me when I went shopping last Saturday."

"You didn't mention that." He wished she had. Every time Janet Bennett wanted anything, Adrienne leaped to help. Riley understood loyalty, but every time Adrienne did anything with her mother, she came back feeling cut down and like a failure as a daughter. Riley liked Janet Bennett just fine. He'd like her even better if she lived on the West Coast, preferably in the earthquake zone. "Forget what your mother said. Take it from me, you look absolutely terrific."

Aware of the time, both automatically moved toward the door, Adrienne snatching her purse and briefcase and Riley toting his luggage. She didn't have to be at work this early, but she could steal a few more minutes with him if she left when he did. "Come on, Riley, you don't have to go overboard. I haven't suddenly become so shallow that I care about looking 'terrific,' but I have to look professional. Burkholtz may have given me a raise, but he hasn't once mentioned the partnership since I told him I was pregnant."

"And one of us in this twosome happens to know labor laws inside out." He locked the door and escorted her down the hall toward the elevator. "If that turkey does anything to imply your pregnancy is an issue affecting your employment—or the partnership—I'll personally take the buzzard to court and hang him out to dry.''

"Calm down," she soothed.

"I know what your work means to you."

"Well, I know how you drive when you're revved up in the morning. Forget Burkholtz and all this other nonsense—it's the last thing you need on your mind." Outside, the summer morning sun was blinding. Once Riley had stashed his suitcase, she reached for him, squinting as she retied his tie. "You're going to have a wonderful time."

"I don't want to go." It was the first chance he'd had to tell her.

"Of course you do." She patted the tie down with a thump but her hands lingered, softly, possessively, on his chest. "You thrive on these things, Riley, and no one's better at them than you are. I'm delighted you have this chance."

"It could still fall through. I'll make calls at the office before I actually take the flight. It's possible they've already settled things."

"And horses can fly. Brown never calls you at six o'clock in the morning unless he has a really good mess for you to wade into," she said humorously. "Heavens, you're not hesitating because of me, are you? I'm thrilled you have this chance to go. How many times do I have to tell you that you can leave me anytime you want to?"

She sounded so thrilled at the thought of him being five thousand miles away that Riley felt kicked, hard.

Maybe he hadn't won last night's war but he'd counting on having won the battle. They'd been as close as a man and woman could be. He couldn't believe she was back to chasing him out of her life again.

He wanted to wrap his arms around her, fold her up, and kiss her so thoroughly that she couldn't see straight. That was what he wanted to do—and what he would have done, if she didn't steal his initiative.

She went up on tiptoe and kissed him, hard. So hard that her tummy rubbed against his belt, he could smell the hint of lavender on her skin, and desire pulled at him. Her lips hovered, then offered a second kiss, this one a tease, a blur of softness and promise.

When she finally pulled back, he felt all the masculine reassurance of having been kissed well and intimately, by a woman who very clearly loved him. That reassurance died when her eyes met his—briefly, fiercely, poignantly. "I want you to take care of yourself, and I want you to have a good time." She barely hesitated. "And if you find someone else, Riley, you're free. You always have been, you always will be. You don't owe me anything and never did."

Hours later, Riley stared blindly out the 747's window. He saw nothing below but a gray, endless Atlantic. Most of the other passengers were napping. He couldn't sleep nor could he concentrate on the contracts on his lap.

Damnation, she *still* thought he was going to stray. Hell, the woman had the same as invited him to find someone else. Maybe he'd been wrong about everything. Maybe she didn't love him, maybe she really didn't want his baby, and maybe it was crazy for him to believe he could sneak a ring on her finger given enough time, patience, love, and yes, dammit, trust.

Maybe he *was* wrong about everything, but every time he closed his eyes, he saw her reaching for him in the night, all passion, all fire. He saw her bearding Brown at the dinner party, listening to his boss's stories so he didn't have to. He saw her ravenously devouring a spinach leaf. He saw her sneaking a peek at the books he'd hidden away. He saw the way she'd looked, hiding in the Browns' bathroom, so upset with herself, so determined he wouldn't know. He saw her soundlessly place a short whiskey on his worktable at the exact instant he was ready to wind down. He saw her—the most beautiful woman alive—the moment she'd felt their baby move.

The pictures hardly added up to a woman in a hurry to end a love affair. He *knew* she loved him. That she wanted both him and the baby. And that if she'd ever needed anyone, she needed him now.

Oh, yeah, Stuart? So why is she halfway to labor and still trying to kick you out the door?

He swiped a hand over his face, feeling exasperated and confused. He had no answers except for the one obvious one. She was frightened. He wasn't giving her up, and Riley reminded himself that he still had months before the baby was born, months to convince her that there was no reason to be scared of him or anything they had together.

That didn't sound so hard. He'd be there when she

needed him. He'd be more patient, more loving, more understanding. He'd be so damned trustworthy that she'd think he was a Boy Scout. He'd woo her until he dropped. And if that didn't work, he could always drag her to the altar, blindfolded and handcuffed. Maybe if the minister did the service in Arabic, she wouldn't realize what it was.

The image momentarily made him smile, but not for long. Adrienne, much as he loved her, could be as stubborn as a mule. And months had a way of flying past faster than the speed of sound.

Chapter Five

"I can't believe how fast the time's gone! Just one more month, Adrienne," Liz said cheerfully. "So, how are we feeling?"

Adrienne mentally rolled her eyes. Liz asked the same question every time, then immediately bent over with a stethoscope hooked in her ears so she couldn't hear a thing. "Just fine," Adrienne murmured in her blithest monotone. "Nothing new. My ankles are swollen. I'm getting varicose veins in my legs. My belly button popped out. Say boo and I cry. I feel ugly, undesirable and klutzy. Two sips of water and I need a bathroom. I could sleep twenty-four hours a day—except at four in the morning, when the baby either gets hiccups or starts kicking—and I only get sick to my stomach three or four times a week now."

Liz lifted her head, pulled the stethoscope out of her ears and smiled. "The baby's doing fine and so are you from the look of you. At the start, I admit I was worried that you wouldn't take care of yourself, but obviously I was wrong. How's Lamaze going?"

"Riley's the ace of the class. He can breathe and pant like nobody's business." Adrienne glanced down at her abdomen, which more and more resembled a small beached whale. She pulled down her blouse and began the long process of shifting from a reclining to a sitting position. A crane would have helped. "He wants to be present at the birth. I don't. I don't suppose we could convince nature to switch things around in our case?"

Liz chuckled.

"How do you feel about drugs?"

"The same way I felt the last time you asked me," the doctor said mildly.

"Well, I still don't see anything wrong with sleeping through the whole process. Whole generations of women had drugs during childbirth—your mom probably did, and I *know* my mother did. Heck, we've overpopulated an entire planet with babies in spite of those drugs." Adrienne finally made it to a sitting position and wagged a finger at her friend. "Do not tell me the pain is an issue of mind over matter or all in the head. I saw the Lamaze movie on childbirth. The pain was not in her head."

"It's over faster than you know. And if it comes to the point where you can't handle it, we'll come through with something to make you more comfortable." Liz shook her head wryly. "I had this same discussion with Riley last week."

Adrienne's head shot up. "What do you mean?"

"Riley's called me once a week from the beginning. Didn't he tell you?"

"No!"

"You mean he didn't talk to you after the last time we did blood work?"

Adrienne's heart stopped with a squeeze. "Was

there something wrong with my blood? Something wrong with the baby you didn't tell me?''

"No, no. That's not why we discussed blood work. I thought you knew—never mind. Riley will tell you. More relevant..." Liz's gaze focused seriously, a doctor suddenly more than a friend. "Are you still working?"

"My leave of absence starts Friday."

Liz looked relieved. "I was afraid you'd taken that partnership, and it's just not the best of times for you to have extra stress."

Riley had said the same thing, but Adrienne was the one who had surprised herself when Burkholtz had finally offered the partnership. She'd not only turned it down but requested a leave. Her work had once meant everything to her. She wasn't sure why, now, she couldn't dredge up an ounce of dedication. "You're sure the baby's all right?"

"The little devil's putting on more weight than you are. My guess is a boy." Liz hesitated. "We're talking a nice big healthy baby, Adrienne, but as we've already discussed, there is a slight chance we may end up doing a cesarean."

"And as we already discussed, that's fine by me. I could just wake up when it's over." Adrienne climbed off the examining table and frowned. "Except that I'd want to know exactly what kind of drugs you use for a cesarean, because if it's anything that could possibly affect the baby—"

"Hey. A moment ago I could have sworn you were bargaining for morphine."

"Oh, shut up, Liz."

Liz chuckled. "Do I need this grief? I've got a whole waiting room of patients who actually thrive on my advice, and here I'm taking my time up with you. Go on, get out of here, but take good care of him, kiddo."

"I thought I was. You said the baby was in great shape."

"The baby is. I was talking about your taking care of Riley." Liz winked.

Adrienne chuckled, but once Liz was gone, her smile folded like a bad poker hand. A small mirror hung over the sink in the examination room. The big-tummied, clumsy, soft-eyed woman in its reflection bore little resemblance to the Adrienne she knew. The Adrienne she knew would never have willingly hurt someone she loved.

She *hadn't* taken care of Riley.

She'd once sworn she'd never tie him down, never corner him with forced responsibilities, yet in the past few months Riley had unquestionably been the one to take care of her.

She'd let that happen—not because she'd suddenly turned into a heartlessly selfish woman, but because this last stretch of pregnancy had been debilitating. Not physically—emotionally. Nature didn't give an owl's hoot about principles. Especially in these past weeks, nature had made very sure that the life growing inside her had dominated everything she did, everything she thought, everything she felt. The overwhelming instinct was to protect the baby from every physical and emotional stress.

Riley hadn't complained. He treated her like coddled treasure, a fragile rose. Riley wasn't a man who ran away from responsibility, but that was just it. She had become a responsibility.

The thought turned her stomach, but the idea that she had been insensitive to Riley's needs made her heart ache. It was about time she faced up to decisions she'd made. It was past time, like Liz said, that she took care of Riley.

"You're sure you're up to this?"

"Positive," Adrienne said gaily.

"It's not like we couldn't have gone tomorrow. With this weather—"

"Now, Riley, it's just a little snow." Actually the November evening was as black as pitch and bleak-cold. The car wipers were going like mad to accommodate the battering spatter of sleet. Riley had only taken her out when she'd insisted...and she'd insisted because she knew he'd wanted this for weeks.

"You're sure you're warm enough?"

"No problem."

"Uncomfortable?"

"Just fine," she fibbed blithely, although the question almost made her laugh. Comfort and a pregnant woman in her eighth month was a contradiction in terms. Her coat no longer buttoned around the middle. Walking was an exercise in waddling. Climbing into the car had a lot in common with stuffing a goose, and Riley had to truss her into the seat belt. She could no longer manage it, particularly after he'd consulted Liz and modified the design to make the seat belt safe for her hippo-sized abdomen.

"Do you have to go to the bathroom?" Riley shot her a grin. "I already know the answer to that one, but we'll be there in another ten minutes."

"I can wait," Adrienne said serenely, but when she glanced at him, she felt guilty for waiting so long. Riley's shoulders were encased in an ancient suede jacket and his dark hair glistened, damp with melting snow. He looked incurably handsome, but even the shadowed car couldn't hide the circles beneath his eyes, his newly honed cheekbones. He'd lost weight in the past months, and his dollop-of-the-devil grins were becoming rare to come by. Her fault.

Well, he was happy tonight—so full of energy he couldn't sit still—and she intended to keep him that way.

Months ago, when Riley had returned from Europe, he'd set the wheels in motion to sever his employment with Brown, hang out his own shingle and go house hunting. Adrienne had supported his break with Brown, knowing how long Riley had wanted to make that move. She'd also enthusiastically gone office shopping with him, and once he found prime rental space, helped him move in and organize.

The house, though, was something else. She knew Riley's plate was too full, yet she'd avoided anything to do with the home he'd finally chosen—a choice that now struck her as selfish and, yes, cowardly. It

wasn't supposed to hurt that he was going to live in
the house with the baby and not her. Why should it?
Both agreed that babies didn't belong with couples
who weren't married. Both were too adult to fall into
the pit of a shotgun marriage, nor was there a need
for it. Riley wanted the baby; she was going to take
the apartment and everything was hunky-dory.

To avoid seeing the house was the same as pretending she was unsure or unhappy or maybe even
feeling devastated about those choices. That wasn't
true, which she intended to prove to him tonight.

Riley turned the corner on a country lane. "You
prepared for a surprise?"

"You bet." What she was really prepared for was
helping him, which she should have done a long time
ago. Riley may not have noticed, but she was dressed
to work. There had to be things she could do. Wash
cupboards? Line shelves?

But her mind blanked when he braked at the end
of a long driveway. The sleety night blurred her vision, but not so much she couldn't see the sprawling
ranch house, the giant fenced yard, the chestnut trees
in the front. All of it should have been unfamiliar. It
wasn't. About a hundred years before they'd taken a
country drive on a lazy Sunday afternoon. "What a
great house for a family," she said then. At the time,
it had been just idle conversation.

Now Adrienne turned stricken eyes to Riley.
"Yeah, I thought you might remember it," he mur-
mured. "Come on, let's get you out of the weather.
I'll put on a pot of coffee while you explore the lay-

out. Only don't expect too much. There's barely a stick of furniture, and I've only had time to have the place repainted and carpeted." He led her up the snowy driveway, and switched on the lights just inside the house. "You're still feeling okay, aren't you?"

"Good enough to climb mountains," she assured him, which wasn't precisely true. He skinned off her coat, put water on the stove and left her to explore. She wished he hadn't. The house was laid out in an L, with the kitchen and living areas in one section, the bedroom wing in another. Maybe the house had no furniture yet, but there were other details to catch her eye.

She'd once said she loved skylights. There were skylights in the kitchen and master bedroom. She'd once said she loved fireplaces. There was a massive fieldstone hearth in the living room and a second smaller fireplace in the master bedroom. The living room was painted cream, the kitchen toast and the carpet Riley had chosen was a thick, plush paprika. Cream, toast and paprika were her favorite colors.

Riley, on stocking feet, stole up behind her with mugs of hot spiced tea. "Like it so far?"

"Very much." That was an understatement. She liked it to the point of pain and despair, but thankfully he didn't seem to realize that. His eyes rested on her face with the gentleness of calm, blue waters, and then he grinned.

"You haven't seen the baby's room yet?"

"No." She didn't want to. She took a bracing sip

of the hot mulled tea and discovered she still didn't want to.

"I'm not sure you should," he admitted ruefully. "It's the worst mess in the whole place."

"It can't be that bad."

"It is."

"Riley..." He wasn't really pushing her toward the door closest to the bathroom, but his knuckle was pressed at the small of her back and he was definitely nudging. He flicked on the overhead switch and there it was.

The baby's room. And damn him, she knew she'd told him she favored yellow for a baby's color, and the room was distinctly painted a soft sunrise yellow. Her throat formed a lump so big she couldn't possibly swallow, not just in reaction to the baby's room but the whole house. She abruptly forced that lump back down.

She'd come to help him, and this was unquestionably the place where he needed it. As he'd said, the room was a total disaster. Every available space was filled with boxes. He'd purchased a crib, playpen, high chair, car seat, stroller and changing table. He just hadn't put any of them together. The job would take a skilled mechanic an entire day.

"I just signed the closing on the house three weeks ago," he defended the debris. "After that...well. You know how busy I've been, and I didn't figure I had to hurry in here with the baby not due for another three or four weeks—"

"Yes." Adrienne gulped another sip of tea. She

had so carefully not involved herself in preparations for the baby, which had seemed a matter of principle. It was Riley's baby, not hers. Not yours, not yours, not yours…the mental echo wailed in her heart like a lost wind, but she banished it as stubbornly as she forced down more tea. It was time to rally, not wallow—and to think of Riley, not herself.

Men invested an enormous amount of masculine ego in being "handy." Riley was a trace touchy on the subject. He should be. The last time he'd picked up a hammer, he'd made a hole in the apartment wall so huge she had to cover it with a picture.

"You know," she said slowly, "I think you and I have really done something special that'll go down in history."

"Pardon?"

"We've managed it. An honest role reversal, à la 1990. You know what I mean. If I'd gotten pregnant fifty years ago, I'd have been 'ruined' if you didn't marry me. Even if I'd become pregnant twenty years ago, I'd have been stuck with the entire responsibility, whether that was right for the baby or not." She'd been wanting to sneak in this little speech for weeks, so she had to talk fast. "Times have changed, for the man as well as the woman, thank heavens. I'm having the child, but you're keeping it, and we were both able to make that decision based on what was right for the child, didn't we? And both of us feel good about it." She smiled at him. "I'm so proud of you— but could you come just a little farther?"

"Beg you pardon?"

"Get me a screwdriver, love."

"What?"

"A screwdriver. Preferably several. A couple of regular and one Phillips head. And throw in an Allen wrench and a hammer?"

"Adrienne..." Whatever he started to say, he seemed to think better of it. He clawed a hand through his hair and sighed. Loudly. "You want to put together the baby's furniture? Now?"

No. If truth were on the line, she wanted nothing to do with the baby's furniture. Rather than touch one oak spindle on the Jenny Lind crib, she'd rather be outside in the sleet, as naked as a jaybird, cavorting around barefoot with her fifty-inch girth and freezing to death.

Dramatically freezing to death, however, would not help Riley. She could handle this. Every instruction she read, every screw she picked up, every fresh mug of tea Riley handed her—she promised herself that she could handle this.

Dammit, she had to.

They finished the crib. One side listed like a drunken sailor. "Only thirteen screws and this strange looking metal thing left over," Riley mentioned dryly.

For the first few minutes he hadn't gotten into it. She'd had to coax and tease—methods that were now, obviously, working too well. "The problem is that I read the directions. Everyone knows they never make any sense. Just hand me that metal part again."

He handed her the metal part. They rebuilt the crib.

She started on the stroller; he started on the high chair. They switched projects midway, both seeking the promised greener grass on the other side of the fence. It wasn't any greener. ''There's nothing sacred about finishing all this stuff tonight,'' Riley kept insisting.

''Now, Riley. You just don't realize how much fun we're having.'' He rolled his eyes, and she had to laugh.

The stroller functioned if you didn't try to lock it. But as far as the playpen... ''For heaven's sake, don't throw away that Easy To Assemble sign on the front of the box,'' Adrienne ordered. ''On that sign alone, we should be able to put the manufacturer behind bars for a good hundred years. Talk about a shut-away case for fraudulent advertising.''

''Adrienne, I know you think you're talented mechanically.'' At that precise moment, they were both sprawled on the floor, back-to-back, their fannies and spines bracing each other. The back of his head leaned against the back of hers, and both of them had their eyes closed. It took too much courage to open them. The whole room was a land mine of cardboard, spare parts, Styrofoam packing material and tools. ''You are good with a screwdriver, I'm not denying it. I just think you take these projects too personally.''

''Of course I do. This is a war. Both of us graduated from law school with honors, for heaven's sake. This is absolutely nothing by comparison.'' Adrienne surged to her feet, no small feat with her bulk, and pushed up the sleeves of her maternity sweater. ''I could handle a hinge cover and drop-rail lock in my sleep.''

''Which is the point. It's eleven o'clock, love.''

''A terrific time to handle—'' she grabbed for an instruction sheet ''—the swivel wheel holder.''

She wasn't really so stubborn. The point was his laughter. Riley hadn't laughed with her—not like this—in ages. Maybe it was late and maybe her back ached. She didn't care. Riley had been increasingly tense for weeks. Tonight the drawn look had disappeared from his eyes and he was relaxed and unquestionably sassy humored.

So was she, until the projects were suddenly done. For a few minutes they busied themselves stuffing Styrofoam and plastic leftovers back into the empty boxes, but then that was done, too.

Silence settled on the softly lit baby's room. A helpless silence. A too-precious-to-breathe silence. Without meaning to, her gaze wandered from the oak crib and high chair to the gay yellow print of the playpen pad. She touched the stroller handle, the shade of the little bedside lamp—it looked like balloons, yellow, red, blue.

''Did we do good or did we do good?'' Riley demanded.

''We did good,'' she whispered, but her voice had an odd watery quality.

''Adrienne?'' He crossed the room in three fast strides, and chucked up her chin too quickly for her to blink back the moisture in her eyes. He sucked in his breath and stood there.

"Everything's fine. I just—"

He didn't give her a chance to finish. "We're leaving. Now."

The snap in his tone startled her. They turned off lights and collected their coats, but it didn't occur to her until they were out in the winter-frosted night that he was bafflingly angry. Riley had never been angry, not at her. It didn't make any sense, but the signs were unmistakable.

Outside, the sleet had stopped. The night was as clear as black ice. He protectively grabbed her arm en route to the car, but once she was installed inside he didn't slam the door. He closed it with a shotgun-sharp little click. And when he turned the key, he glanced at her. He looked as if he wanted to get his hands around her throat. For eight months he'd been treating her like fragile china.

"You're going to have to tell me what's wrong, because I don't have any idea," she said quietly.

"Nothing's wrong. You warm enough?"

It was a relative question. The heater was going full blast, but the emotional temperature in the car threatened frost. "Something upset you," she persisted.

"Forget it."

She wanted to. She was cold and uncomfortable and tired. The closer she came to the end of this pregnancy, the more she felt fragile and scared and wary of walking into anything she couldn't handle. Riley looked as manageable as a two-hundred-pound stick of just-lit dynamite, and the alluring temptation was to ignore the problem until he'd calmed down. *Like you've ignored everything else, Adrienne?* "I want to know what upset you," she insisted.

"No, you don't."

"Come on, Riley. I'm not a cupcake. I don't crumble. If I said something to upset you, I want to know it!"

"You said—and did—things that upset me, all right." On the freeway, Riley changed lanes with caution and care, but on the inside, he was losing it. "All that business about role reversals à la 1990. About how values have finally, really changed for both men and women. About our having the freedom to make the *right* decisions about the baby's future. Maybe you could sell that con to a used-car salesman, Adrienne, but you're through selling it to me."

"What?"

"I bought the house for you, because you loved it on sight. You may not have seen the inside until tonight, but you loved it on sight, too. And no, don't start talking yet. Just answer me. Did you or did you not like the house?"

There was only one answer she could give him. "I loved it," she admitted softly.

"Yeah. Only I thought when you were willing to see it that you were finally..." He shifted gears. "Dammit, I've always understood that you had real, honest reasons to be wary of marriage. Watching your parents' relationship had to be a little bit of hell when you were growing up, and everything in your job has to underline the same messages. You see people hurting each other, relationships not making it, commitments abandoned faster than the change of seasons.''

She could feel her face blanching of color. ''Riley—''

His eyes leveled on her for bare seconds, as blue as ice. ''I'm not responsible for all those other people, brown eyes. Just for me, and I know damn well how I feel—about us, about you, about commitment. I *love you*, and I'm tired as hell of your thinking I'm going to cut out on you at the first sign of rough waters.''

She couldn't think when he was shouting. ''Riley, you're not being fair. I never thought...'' She hesitated. ''Maybe when I first met you, I did. Believe you'd leave me at the first slam of a door. But believe me, that hasn't been true for a long time.''

''No?'' he demanded.

''No.''

''You've actually come to trust me?''

Trust? There was a time the five-letter word hadn't been in her vocabulary, but that was before this pregnancy. For the past eight months Riley had been there for her—even when she was chasing him away, even when she'd been such a pill she'd have walked out on herself.

''Adrienne?''

She closed her eyes. ''I wasn't hesitating for lack of an answer. I was just trying to find some way to answer you that didn't sound hopelessly corny. I don't want to embarrass you, counselor, but I'd trust you with my life.''

She'd hoped her answer meant something to him,

but Riley clammed up with a frown. Within minutes, they were parked outside the apartment. It was so cold that the windows started fogging up the moment he shut off the engine, isolating the two of them in the dark car. When she reached for the door handle, though, his hand clamped on her wrist.

"You trust me, Adrienne. And I think you love me. So I'll be damned if I can understand why we're not married."

She felt cornered, not so much by his hand on her wrist as his gaze. Everywhere she looked Riley's eyes were waiting for her, determined and harsh and demanding. "You haven't asked me to marry you," she said unsteadily, "at least from the start of this pregnancy."

Riley saw the prick of emotional tears in her eyes. Still he pressed. "Because you'd have bitten my head off. But you knew it was what I wanted." When she tried to avert her head, he cupped her chin in his gloved hand. She knew. "Maybe you'll never stop being wary of the institution, but you stopped being wary of me and what we have together a long time ago. I think you want a marriage as much as I do."

"No. You know how I feel about marriage."

"I know what you *say*. Just like I know what you *say* about the baby. You still think you plan to take a fast boat to China the minute the baby's born, and I think it's time we cleared up that horse manure. You should have seen your face when you touched that crib tonight. You want this baby so badly it's eating you up inside—it's on your mind day and night."

"No!"

"Yes." His hands closed on her shoulders. His face was gaunt, and the hollows beneath his eyes dark. "All this time I thought it was me you were afraid of, but it's the baby, isn't it? You're so scared of this baby that you can't think straight, and I have no possible way to understand that unless you talk to me. Why, Adrienne? It's a baby we both want and both love, so why is it tearing you apart?"

"Riley, leave it be!" He grabbed her arm again, but she managed to wrench open the door and stumble out. She had never so desperately needed to be alone, just for a minute, just long enough to escape the smothering small car and Riley's relentless questions.

Cold air slammed into her lungs and froze the tears on her cheeks, and she suddenly hurt everywhere; inside, outside, all over.

He didn't come after her. It was an hour later—she was curled up in bed with her eyes wide open on the ceiling—before she heard his key in the lock. Another hour passed and he still hadn't come near her.

Confused and lost, she stared in the darkness until she was positive he was asleep in the other room. Still, it took her a long time to find the strength to do what she had to do. She felt sure of nothing...except that she'd hurt Riley enough.

Chapter Six

She wasn't running away. Maybe she'd taken off at three in the morning without a stitch of luggage, but that hardly meant she was running away. She'd left Riley a note so he wouldn't worry; it was hardly criminal to need some time to herself, and it wasn't as though she didn't know where she was going.

At least, she decided where she was going as soon as she stopped at a gas station, which happened quickly. Predictably her fuel tank was on Empty. The station obligingly provided machines where she could pick up a cardboard container of milk, and more relevant, maps.

There were other choices, but it was the map of the Ozarks that captured her attention. She had a sudden memory of the greens and quiet and peaceful dark woods from a childhood vacation in the mountains. It seemed an ideal place to calm down and think through her decisions in the weeks before the baby was born.

No matter which route she took, it was an enormously long drive. She told herself it didn't matter. The farther the better. She could always stop at a motel when she tired, and maybe she wasn't loaded with cash, but her wallet had half a dozen credit cards and a padded checkbook.

The dark night spit snow as she crossed the Indiana border into Illinois, and the blacktop loomed ahead of her, endless and bleak. Her abdomen rested against the steering wheel and the weight ached, but it troubled her that the baby didn't kick tonight. Because mature, grown women didn't run away?

So we're dealing with your basic immature coward, little one. Just goes to show I was never the mother for you.

She nearly missed the turnoff for Route 72 because her vision was blurred by tears. Riley didn't understand. He thought she loved him. He thought she wanted to marry him. He thought she wanted the baby.

Dammit, he was right about all of that, but he didn't *understand*. She had no business having a baby; she never had. If Riley loved her, he had fallen in love with the Adrienne he thought she was: a career woman, competent and independent, self-reliant and sure of herself. Before the pregnancy Adrienne had been just that, but she'd had eight-plus months to remember that she was unalterably, undeniably her mother's daughter.

Adrienne had figured out a long time ago that Janet Bennett was a woman who couldn't love or be loved. As a child, Adrienne had been hurt by her mother's insensitivity. As an adult, she'd buried the old hurts and responded with sympathy for a woman so lonely, so lost.

But since the pregnancy, she'd been the one to feel lonely and lost. She had her mother's genes and couldn't seem to forget it. Self-reliance and competence were tricks to survival, but there'd never been confidence under the surface. Fear of losing Riley had always affected her being honest with him about who she really was, who she wanted to be. And what if she turned out to be a mother like her own was? How could she risk doing that to Riley's baby?

That's no excuse for running away, ducky.

But I was so scared.

You should be. You're about to lose a man who means the world to you and a baby more precious than life. Is that what you want?

I'm afraid...

Is that what you want?

What if I'm a terrible mother? You don't understand how I feel about Riley's baby. How could I possibly risk hurting his child?

Is that what you want? To lose him?

The first hundred miles rushed past, then another hundred. She stopped every hour to find a gas station rest room, and little cardboard containers of milk started to accumulate on the seat beside her.

On every lonely stretch of blacktop, her mind played through long buried insecurities and ancient fears. For centuries women had taken childbirth for granted. It wasn't that way anymore. These were contemporary times. A woman was no longer stuck. She had the choice to do what was right, for her baby, for herself. That's all Adrienne had ever wanted. To do what was right. For Riley, for herself, for the baby.

Her baby.

Mine.

The rush and power of that sweet word took her heart, captured it, wouldn't let go. If love meant anything at all, they were both hers. Riley and the baby.

By the time she crossed into Missouri, she would have given a year of her life to be able to turn around and go home, but it wasn't that easy. She'd come too far to backtrack the entire distance at a stretch, and Riley wouldn't be awake yet. By the time he was, she planned to be stopped and near a telephone.

For the moment she was in the middle of nowhere. It was past dawn but still gloomy. The sun had risen behind a sky mottled with charcoal clouds. Sleet had dulled into a steady driving rain, and winter-barren grain fields stretched for long rolling miles. One farmer's pickup passed her, but that was the only traffic on the road except for the dark car far behind her.

For the third time, she glanced in the rearview mirror. Riley had a dark four-door. More by accident than intention, her feet let up on the gas pedal. When she slowed down to five miles an hour, the car behind her also slowed down. Deliberately she floored the accelerator. The other driver must have responded by flooring his, because the distance between them was kept exactly the same.

She lost sight of her shadow on a curve, but as soon as she reached a straightaway he was there again. The car never came so close that she could see the driver or identify the car's make. Still, it wasn't really a shadow and it wasn't really Riley. Her imagination was running away from her because he was on her mind—desperately, invasively and lovingly on her mind. *I'm not losing you, Riley. I can't. I won't.*

She was running low on gas when the first cramp cut off her breath. Her first reaction was terror, but that faded quickly. It couldn't be the baby because it couldn't be labor. Not only was the baby not due for three weeks, but labor didn't start like this. She'd read all Riley's hidden books and taken the Lamaze class. Labor started with slow, far apart little twinges that gradually built up into serious cramps. Even if it were the baby, heaven knew she had time. According to the books, especially with a first birth, it could be hours before anything really started happening.

Five minutes later, an invisible vise clamped on her abdomen so hard that her brow broke sweat.

So much for the books.

When Riley saw her car swerve, a ribbon of ice coiled around his heart. He severed the distance between them with his foot flat on the gas. When she pulled off onto the wide shoulder, he was right behind her. She hadn't fully stopped before he jerked his door open.

Wind beat at him as he ran toward her car. Rain ran through his hair, cold and slick and unnoticed. He lost ten years of his life when he looked through the windshield. Adrienne's chestnut head was leaned over the steering wheel; she was limp and still.

Riley didn't start breathing again until he'd wrenched open her door. She turned her head then, saw him and blindly held out her arms. Her eyes were so clotted with thick, soft tears that she turned his entire heart inside out. "Riley, I'm sorry. I've been so stupid, and I know I've put you through hell."

As if he cared. She was alive and okay. He pulled her out of the car—to hell with the pouring rain—and kissed her. And kissed her. And kissed her. He wanted to tell her that he'd shoot her if she ever ran away from him again, but somehow he couldn't work up the anger. She tasted like lost treasure, now found. She smelled like lavender. And her lips were warm under his, wooing warm, heart warm, Adrienne warm.

He felt life flood back through his body—life that had been cold and dead when he'd heard her leave the apartment. Her response had nothing to do with passion and everything to do with love, a love so deep she never felt the rain, so deep that her fingers clutched his hair as if she'd never let him go. And he would probably have kissed her from here to forever if she hadn't suddenly leaned back and doubled over.

"What the—"

"The baby."

He froze on the bleat of a heartbeat. *"Now?"*

"Now, love. I think we'd better find a doctor, Riley."

She smiled at him, all calm and loving. She'd been the frantic one all these months, now it was him. He hustled her into the passenger seat of her car, started the engine and immediately saw she had no gas. In no crisis in her life did Adrienne ever have gas. He grabbed her car key, purse and her, and jogged them back to his car. His hands were slick on the wheel as he floored the accelerator. The last sign he saw had been for the town of Hannibal. That had been miles back. There were no towns on this stretch of highway. And Adrienne would not be in labor if he hadn't started the argument earlier that night.

"Riley..."

She started to talk, then closed her eyes and clamped her teeth together. She was the one in pain, but his whole forehead was sheened with sweat and his heart galloped in his chest. He held on to the steering wheel hard enough to break it. Junction 10 Miles said the sign, which also pictured gas and thank heavens a medical facility.

"Riley, I want your baby. I always did."

"Sweetheart, I know that."

"I was just so afraid of being a mother like mine was. I spent a childhood believing I was just like her."

"Honey, you never had more in common with your mother than a turkey. Please don't do that. How the hell often are those pains coming?"

"I don't know. Four, five minutes."

He pushed down the gas pedal.

"Riley...I worked so hard for my career, for that partnership—and it hasn't meant a bite of fudge in months. It doesn't matter like I thought it did. I have to tell you—I *need* to tell you—that I'm not the career woman you fell in love with. I—"

"Honey, breathe. In. Out."

"I want...to be home. I want to diaper and feed my own baby and I don't want any stranger seeing its first steps. I want to be a chocolate-chip cookie maker of a mother. I know that sounds corny, and I was always afraid you'd never be attracted to an old-fashioned housewife. But if I had my choice, if I ever just had one chance to be the woman I want to be…I want to make a family like the one I never had, to do it right, to give it everything I have—"

"Adrienne?"

"Hmm?"

"I don't care if you work for the rest of your life, love. I never did. You can work. You can be at home. Either way I always figured you'd love the baby from here to forever, so I don't see a problem. Whatever you want's fine. Except that I'd really appreciate it, love. I would really appreciate it if you'd stop the damned labor pains until I've found a hospital."

She made a sound. It wasn't a scream. It was just a sound coming out of her throat that had something of horrified surprise. She wasn't just hurting. She was dying of pain.

He reached Junction and pulled off to find a sleepy farming town with a farm store, an implement dealer, a grocery store, and unbelievably far down the road, a two-story redbrick building with a sign, Junction General Hospital. The sign was nearly bigger than the place, and the place looked pretty archaic to Riley, but he wasn't floating around with choices.

"Riley?"

"Ssh."

"That last one hurt." But she smiled.

He didn't. Lifting her out of the car, he was in the

mood to kill someone. Adrienne was not only exhausted but weak, her eyes dazed with pain. She cramped up again just as he was barreling through the double doors.

A young woman with braided blond hair smiled a greeting at him from the reception desk. She wasn't smiling long.

"I want your entire surgical team," he told her. "Anesthesiologists. Your best OBY-GYN man. A pediatrician. Internist, surgeon—the whole team."

"That's very nice, sir, but could I have your Blue Cross card? I can see she's in labor, but I can't admit her without a—"

"Where the Sam Hill is the delivery room?"

"Upstairs, sir, but I can't admit her without—"

He balanced Adrienne's rear end on the counter, threw the stupid woman his entire wallet and strode toward the elevator.

"Riley, I can walk," Adrienne whispered.

"Ssh." He kissed her, on the brow, on the cheek, fleetingly, tenderly. Then, in his arms, she folded toward him with yet another contraction. It had to take five years for the wheezing elevator to arrive on the second floor.

When the doors finally opened, he strode out with the speed of a cavalry charge, only to find a tomb-quiet corridor painted a pale, dead green. The only sign of life was a gray-haired nurse with the build of a drill sergeant, bending over some forms at a desk. She glanced up. "She's having a baby," he snapped.

"Yes, I can see that."

"The first thing you have to do is put her out of pain. She's hurting. Dammit, do something!"

"My, my, we seem a little distraught—"

"I'm not distraught. I'm mad as hell. Give her something!"

"Riley, you have to calm down, and for heaven's sake put me down before you break your back," Adrienne said firmly.

"Ssh." He kissed her again, lips molded on her brow, but his eyes met the gray-haired battle-ax with fire. "The baby's three weeks early. I want the best doctors flown in from wherever in the country, and more immediately I want drugs. Any of them. All of them. I want her out of pain, you got that? Now!"

The elevator doors cranked open and the young receptionist sprinted out. "Mary, she's not admitted. This man just—"

"It's all right. We'll get it all taken care of," Mary said calmly.

"He didn't sign—"

"I heard you, Anne. Just leave the admitting form on my desk and go back downstairs. I'll handle it." Mary motioned Riley down the hall to the last room on the left, but her shrewd eyes were on her patient. "What's you name, dear?"

As Adrienne exchanged names, she felt the nurse's blunt, strong hand enclose hers. The woman's touch was a woman's bond. Fear, unacknowledged, ebbed out of her. Maybe she was exhausted and the contractions bewilderingly strong and fast, but there was a secret bubble inside her as strong as excitement, as huge as happiness.

"How often, dear?"

"Erratic. But I think around every four minutes."

"Water break?"

"No."

"Anything I need to know about? RH factor, high blood pressure? Anything unusual in the pregnancy, or a reason to expect a difficult delivery?"

"No, everything's been fine until now—except that Liz, my doctor, was a little concerned that the baby was of a size…" A cramp seized Adrienne, hard and sharp. Mary timed it.

"Rough one?" she asked sympathetically.

"A little."

"A little! That's what they've been like for an hour!" Riley snapped to the nurse. He didn't like the room. There was nothing in it but a pristine single bed, table and chair. It smelled sterile and it looked cold. "We need a doctor."

"She'll have a doctor, as soon as we have something to report to him." Mary took a pulse and blood pressure, checking the baby's heartbeat, and then smoothly and efficiently helped Adrienne out of her clothes and folded her into bed. "I'm going to examine you. It'll be a little uncomfortable, but it only takes a moment and then we'll know how dilated you are." She spoke to Adrienne, but her flat, blunt hand was on Riley's chest. He seemed to be moving backward toward the door.

"Forget it. I'm not leaving her."

"There now, I won't argue with you," Mary said pleasantly. "Right past the nurses' station is a waiting room. I just made a fresh pot of coffee. You just pour yourself a nice big mug, and once I've had a chance to examine your wife and page the doctor, you can come right back in here."

"I don't want coffee. I just want…" Riley looked past her shoulder at Adrienne.

"I'll be fine," Adrienne promised him.

Mary firmly closed the door, and talked calmly and gently through the short examination. "As I'm sure you noticed, we're not a metropolitan-size facility, but that's not to say you're not in fine hands. Doc Henley was called downstairs—dreadful accident on the highway this morning—but I'll have him up here soon enough. You'll love him, everyone does, but just so you know, I've have five babies of my own, and delivered more babies out of my room 232 here than I can count. Everything's going to be just fine."

She leaned back up, peeled off her glove and reached for the fetal monitor. Within seconds, she had the steady flow of a readout. "That baby's in fine position—absolutely no sign of stress—and you're dilated a full five centimeters. That means you have another five to go, dear, and the best thing you can do for both you and the baby is to rest between contractions."

"Riley—"

"Yes. Riley," Mary murmured dryly. "All in all, I have the feeling you're going to make it through this a great deal easier than your husband."

Adrienne's voice had a catch. "He's not…my husband."

"Well, now…" Mary, unconcerned, covered Adrienne with a cool, smooth sheet. "Some people have always taken a little longer than others to take care of that detail."

"He's so upset—"

Mary nodded. "Try not to worry. I've been nursing for almost twenty-five years and never lost a father yet." She checked the monitor one last time, pulled the shades and moved toward the door. "I'll send in an aide with some ice chips, but after that you just rest until the doctor comes. And I won't be any farther away than that page button if you want me."

"Mary?"

"Yes, dear."

"Are you going to send Riley back in?"

"Once he's calmed down, yes, if you want him."

"I want him." Her heart was in her voice. "You have no idea how much I want him," she whispered fiercely.

The waiting room was painted the same sick green as the halls. Decorations included three Naugahyde chairs, a clanking radiator, a needlepoint picture of a redbrick town hall, and some farming magazines on a well-nicked table. All in all it was an innocuous room. Riley saw it as a torture chamber. He was dragging a hand through his hair for the hundredth time when the stout nurse reappeared in the doorway.

"What took you so long? Is she all right? Is the baby all right? Can I go back in there?"

Mary motioned him to follow her out to the hall to her desk. "The doctor's already been in and gone. She's fine, the baby's fine, and the contractions have let up for a bit. She's catching a ten-minute catnap and she needs it." She took the seat behind her desk and motioned Riley to the chair beside it. "You and I have a few things we need to take care of, and now's a very good time."

The admitting form only needed his signature where she'd marked an X. She'd taken addresses and insurance information from his wallet, which she now tried to hand back to him. He stared at her blankly. With a sigh, she bent low over her bottom drawer and straightened with a half-full bottle of whiskey and a shot glass. She'd seen expectant fathers in worse shape, but not many. His shirt was buttoned wrong; his eyes were bloodshot with panic and anxiety; and he barely glanced at her when she folded his fingers around the shot glass.

"This is all my fault," he said bleakly.

"You think so? In my part of the country, it takes two."

"You don't understand. I started an argument. She was perfectly fine before that. It's my fault she's in labor." The nurse pantomimed his downing the shot glass. "I love her."

"I can see that." When he'd gulped it, she recapped the bottle and packed it neatly back in her bottom drawer.

Riley patted his pocket and drew out a worn sheet of paper. "It's a marriage license. You know how long I've been carrying this around?"

"Tell me," Mary encouraged calmly.

"Liz—that's her doctor—fixed up the blood work, and that's what I was trying to talk to Adrienne about last night. Not the blood work. Getting married. Only she doesn't want to marry me, and I..." The whiskey hit him like a slam, first blurring his vision and then clearing it. He focused on Mary as if she were a total stranger, which she was. "I don't know what I'm talking to you for. I'm going back in there with her."

"I think you should," Mary agreed.

When he pelted down the hall, she glanced at the worn sheet he'd laid on her desk, forgotten. She studied it for a moment and then reached for the phone.

Riley looked so worn when he walked through the door; so worn, so frightened, so dear. Adrienne lifted her hand and he took it. His palm was like ice, but his eyes had never been more warm or blue. "Riley, please stop worrying. It's going to be okay."

She looked so small and fragile that he had to lean over and kiss her. "We'll make it okay." Because she was so calm and sure, he even started to believe it. At least he smiled, suddenly, for the first time in hours. "Hey. When'd you get so beautiful?" he murmured.

She chuckled. An hour passed, and then another before her contractions picked up momentum again. The first ones were fleabites by comparison.

"Breathe, Riley," she scolded. "In and out, little puffs. You can do it."

That made him laugh, and the sterile, cold room 232 slowly warmed, became an enclave of two. He fed her ice chips, rubbed her back. She told him bad jokes and they both tolerated the regular arrival of Mary, who seemed to think Adrienne needed regular examinations and a report. "Six centimeters." "Seven. Won't be long now, you two!"

For Adrienne's sake, Riley wanted it over. For his own, there was a growing, incomparable magic seeping into this room. Nothing in his life compared. He'd never felt closer to Adrienne, never imagined that intimacy could have this dimension. Their baby was on its way. Their baby. Not a damn thing in the whole world mattered but this, but her.

Adrienne had been hearing war stories about labor for months. The truth was worse than the stories and exhaustion had become her worst enemy, yet she found herself praying not yet. When it was over, she could never have this moment back with Riley. He was afraid, she knew, and it was the first time since she'd known him that she could be there for him. He needed her. Not the other way around. He needed her—she could feel it, see it, taste it.

"What's wrong with Archibald?" he teased.

"The same thing that's wrong with Hortense. Could you please get serious here?"

"All right, all right. Harold. George. Rudolph. Frederick."

"No, times four. What do you think about your own name?"

"A Riley junior? You'd do that to my son? And I thought I loved you."

The next contraction hit with shattering power. Adrienne forgot about breathing and grabbed on to his hand. Sweat coated her whole body with a fine glaze, and Riley kept counting, counting, counting, promising it would be over...and then it was. She opened her eyes, saw the fierce love in his and whispered, "I'm in trouble."

He instantly jerked up from the chair. "I knew it had to be near time. I'll get Mary, the doctor, the whole damn staff—"

"Ssh. Not that kind of trouble. Or yes...just that kind of trouble, but not quiet yet. Listen to me, Riley."

"Honey, if you—"

"Please listen." It had been an enormous relief to confess her fears and feelings to him—her fears about being a good mother, her feelings about the kind of woman she wanted to be. But she had more to confess than that, a far greater mountain to risk, and she knew she was running out of time. "Through it all, Riley," she said softly, "through biting your head off whenever you mentioned rings, through being grumpy and moody and nasty—"

"Sweetheart, you weren't—"

"Yes, I was. I made too much of a childhood I should have outgrown. I said I didn't trust you, when it was myself I was afraid to trust. What I want you to know, though, is that through it all I loved you. I've always loved you. I was unsure about a hundred things, but never that.''

''How much?''

''Pardon?'' The declaration had come from her heart, past every fear of rejection, past every milestone of caution she had ever emotionally erected. Somehow she expected him to react a little differently than to jerk off the bed with a rocket's energy and the devil's gleam in his eyes.

''How much do you love me? Enough to take a chance? Enough to marry me?''

Her soothing ''Yes'' was intended to calm him. Riley responded as though a fire was licking at his heels. ''Don't you dare change your mind,'' he ordered her, smacked a kiss on her forehead and barreled out the door. Down the hall she heard him shouting for Mary.

Mary took care of gowning both men in the scrub room. She was fussy, insisting on the cap and booties and supervising their hands washing as if they were children. Riley was ready first; she sent him through the door where Dr. Henley was already with Adrienne.

Reverend Miller moved slower. Nearing seventy, he wasn't used to being rushed from his lunch. ''You've called me at all hours, Mary, but I have to say never for this.''

''When you've been a nurse as long as I have, you learn to be prepared for anything,'' Mary said mildly.

"You told him the license was no good? That the Indiana license isn't valid in Missouri?"

"Of course I didn't tell him that. A marriage in front of God is what counts and besides, they can take care of that legal business any old time. Only if you don't hurry up, Hiram, it's going to be too late. I told you she was already fully dilated—"

Hiram took a long, pompous breath. "It's possible I might have a slight queasy stomach. I've never seen a baby born."

"Well, at your age, it's about time," Mary scolded. "And you're not going to faint. You're not going to have time. You've got both a wedding and a christening to perform—the most efficient piece of work you've done in a long time. Now get in there!"

The minister walked through, took one look at the scene in the operating room, ducked his head fast to the open Bible in his hands and stuttered out a rapid, "Dearly Beloved…"

Mary had her hands full. The baby's head was crowning before the first "I do." Hiram tried to go weak-kneed on her; her patient was exhausted; the doctor was in Riley's way—both of them wanted to catch the baby. John David was born to the musical crescendo of clanging radiators and a last "I do," and then there was the christening.

Mary didn't like confusion in her operating room, never tolerated it, and annoying her further were the tears in her eyes. She'd seen far too much life to become emotional at her seasoned age. The miracle of love and life, though…she never tired of it. These

two were just starting the cycle, beginning the ultimate romance of a life together.

They say times had changed. Mary knew better.

"What are you doing, Riley?"

"Kissing the bride."

"I think you should unwrap him again and recount
his toes. Are you sure?"

"I'm sure. He's perfect."

"He looks red and squished to me."

"He's perfect."

"Yes," she breathed. Every time she blinked away
the tears, there was a new batch. If her heart felt
fulller, it would probably burst. Their son was tucked
at her side; he was warm and perfect and alive and
beautiful. So was her new husband of less than thirty
minutes, who was leaning over her with an extremely
silly smile on his face. Riley's eyes were possessive,
proud, loving—a little fierce—and nothing was budg-
ing that grin of his. "We could have waited," she
murmured.

"For the marriage? You have to be kidding, love.
I don't often catch you in a weak moment. I couldn't
risk your changing your mind."

"You're out of luck, Mr. Stuart. Nothing this side
of the earth was going to change my mind about mar-
rying you. You're stuck with me."

"Are we talking stuck like glue, Mrs. Stuart?"

"We're talking forever, Riley."

"It took you long enough to believe in it," he murmured, and kissed her again. The kiss was a seal and a vow.

She returned the same seal with her lips, the same vow with her eyes, the same love with her heart.

*   *   *   *   *

Danger, deception and desire

▼™ SILHOUETTE
INTRIGUE ™

Enjoy these dynamic mysteries with a
thrilling combination of breathtaking
romance and heart-stopping suspense.
Unexpected plot twists and
page-turning writing will keep you
on the edge of your seat.

Four new titles every month
available from the
Reader Service ™

SILHOUETTE
SPECIAL EDITION ®

Satisfying, substantial and compelling romances packed with emotion.

Experience the drama of living and loving in the depth and vivid detail that only Special Edition™ can provide. The sensuality can be sizzling or subtle but these are always very special contemporary romances.

Six new titles available every month from the

Reader Service™